Damian's Blood Moon

by

Jamie scott

Dedications

To my younger self, the one who devoured fantasy novels under the covers with a flashlight, who dreamt of epic battles and impossible magic, and who believed, with unwavering conviction, that anything was possible. This book is a testament to that boundless imagination, a reminder that even the most fantastical dreams can take flight, given enough courage, perseverance, and a healthy dose of caffeine. It's a tribute to the power of stories to transport us to other worlds, to ignite our passions, and to inspire us to become the heroes of our own narratives.

This is also dedicated to all those who have ever felt like an outsider, like they didn't quite fit in, like they were carrying a hidden power, a secret destiny, waiting to be unleashed. This story is for you – a reminder that your perceived weaknesses might actually be your greatest strengths, that your differences are what make you extraordinary, and that your unique path, however winding or unpredictable it may seem, is ultimately the one you were meant to walk.

To every reader who ever lost themselves in the pages of a book, who felt the chill of a ghostly encounter, the thrill of a daring escape, the heartache of a lost love, the exhilaration of a hard-fought victory: this book is for you. May it transport you to a world of werewolves, ancient prophecies, and fierce battles, where the line between good and evil blurs, and the ultimate triumph rests not on strength alone, but on the courage to embrace the unknown, the resilience to overcome adversity, and the unwavering belief in the power of one's own destiny. May it ignite your imagination, awaken your spirit, and leave you breathless with wonder and excitement.

Finally, this book is for the countless individuals who have supported me on my own journey – my family, my friends, my mentors, and my fellow writers. Your encouragement, your belief in me, and your unwavering support have been the wind beneath my wings, the fuel for my fire, and the guiding stars that illuminated my path. This achievement is as much yours as it is mine. Thank you. Without you, this story would never have been written. May this book resonate with you in some small way, and may it remind you of the incredible power of belief, hope, and the unwavering pursuit of one's dreams.

Thank you so very much Michelle Estor for all that you do, especially on the cover art, it's so amazing.

Table of Contents

Chapter 1

Chapter 2:

Chapter 3:

Chapter 4:

Chapter 5:

Chapter 6:

Chapter 1
The Blood Moon Prophecy

The scent of freshly baked bread and woodsmoke hung heavy in the air, a familiar comfort in the small town of Oakhaven. Sixteen-year-old Damian inhaled deeply, the familiar aroma grounding him in a life that felt both ordinary and strangely...off. He lived with the Millers, a kind, older couple who'd taken him in as a baby, their love unwavering and unconditional. Their modest farmhouse, nestled amongst rolling hills, was his sanctuary, a place of warmth and laughter that had always felt like home. Yet, even in this idyllic setting, a sense of unease, a subtle dissonance, often hummed beneath the surface.

He'd always been different, he knew that. Even as a child, sleep was rarely restful. His dreams were vivid, chaotic tapestries of shadows, snarling beasts, and a blood-red moon that seemed to pulse with an ominous energy. He'd often wake with a pounding heart, his breath ragged, the lingering taste of iron on his tongue, a feeling he couldn't quite explain. These dreams had become more frequent, more intense, as his sixteenth birthday approached.

The Millers, bless their hearts, attributed these episodes to a vivid imagination, a quirky characteristic they affectionately indulged. They didn't pry, never questioned the inexplicable fears that sometimes gripped him, the strange urges that occasionally surged through his veins—a feeling of wildness, of untamed power simmering just beneath the skin. They loved him, and that was all that mattered.

His days were filled with the rhythm of small-town life: helping Mr. Miller with chores on their farm, sharing jokes with Mrs. Miller over a cup of tea, hanging out with his best friends, Maya and Liam. Maya, with her infectious laugh and boundless energy, was his confidante, the one person who could always make him smile, even when his unsettling dreams had left him feeling exhausted and on edge. Liam, quiet and observant, was the steady anchor in his life, a loyal friend who always had his back.

Their friendship was a bedrock, a grounding force amidst the creeping unease that had begun to shadow his existence. They spent their days exploring the woods surrounding Oakhaven, climbing trees, swimming in the nearby creek, sharing secrets and dreams under the canopy of leaves. Those carefree days seemed to hold a bittersweet poignancy now, a stark contrast to the destiny that awaited him.

He'd never known his biological parents, a mystery the Millers were strangely reticent about. The vague details they offered – a tragic accident, a sudden disappearance – were shrouded in an air of secrecy. There was a sadness in their eyes when the topic arose, a quiet understanding that some stories were best left untold. He'd accepted their explanation, their love a sufficient answer to the unanswered questions that gnawed at his heart.

Yet, sometimes, whispers of the supernatural would weave their way into his ordinary existence. Strange occurrences, things that defied logic, began to pepper his seemingly normal life. The wind would howl with an unnatural intensity, trees would creak and groan as if burdened by some unseen weight, and shadows seemed to lengthen and darken, morphing into grotesque shapes in the periphery of his vision. The animals, too, reacted strangely to his presence; the usually timid rabbits would freeze in his path, their eyes wide with an inexplicable fear, while the crows would caw with an unsettling intensity, their black wings beating a rhythm of foreboding.

There were other, subtler anomalies. He noticed a peculiar sensitivity to moonlight, feeling an almost physical pull towards its ethereal glow. The full moon, in particular, seemed to ignite something within him, a surge of raw energy that left him restless, agitated, filled with a potent, primal power he couldn't comprehend. And yet, he dismissed it all as mere coincidence, as the ramblings of an overactive imagination fueled by late-night readings of gothic novels.

The bond he shared with the Millers was deep, a tapestry woven with years of shared laughter, quiet moments, and a love that felt as solid and comforting as the ancient oak trees that surrounded their home. They were his family, the only family he'd ever known, and their affection was a warm shield against the uncertainty that occasionally threatened to engulf him. But the shadow of his unknown heritage, of a destiny he couldn't yet fathom, loomed ever larger, its presence becoming more pronounced as his sixteenth birthday drew closer.

His sixteenth birthday was celebrated with a simple dinner, a small gathering of close friends and family. The Millers had prepared his favorite meal: roast chicken, mashed potatoes, and a decadent chocolate cake. The atmosphere was filled with warmth and laughter, a stark contrast to the growing unease that thrummed within him. Later, as he retired to his room, a peculiar sense of foreboding enveloped him. The night outside was exceptionally still, the air thick with an almost tangible energy. He looked out the window and saw it: a blood moon, a crimson orb hanging heavy in the inky sky, its malevolent glow casting long, distorted shadows across his room.

It was then, amidst the ominous glow, that he found it—a hidden compartment behind a loose brick in his bedroom fireplace. Inside, nestled within a worn leather-bound journal, was the truth. A truth that would irrevocably shatter his peaceful existence, a truth that would plunge him into a world of werewolves, ancient prophecies, and a destiny he never asked for but could no longer ignore.

The journal, filled with faded ink and brittle pages, detailed his family history, a lineage steeped in the ancient lore of werewolves. He learned of the Alpha lineage, a bloodline passed down through generations, and that he, Damian, was the rightful heir, the next

Alpha of the Silvermoon Pack. He was meant to lead his people, guide them through the shadows, protect them from the dangers that lurked in the darkness. A wave of nausea washed over him, the weight of this revelation crushing him beneath its gravity. He was no ordinary teenager; he was the prophesied Alpha, destined to transform into the most powerful werewolf under the blood moon's ominous glow.

The journal also revealed the threat that loomed over him, a threat that had followed his family for generations: Keegan, his ruthless uncle, the leader of a rival werewolf clan known as the Shadowfang Pack. Keegan desired the Alpha's power, the strength and influence that came with the title, and he would stop at nothing to seize it, even if it meant eliminating Damian, his own nephew. The chilling detail that stood out, etched permanently in his mind, was that should Damian die before the blood moon rose, Keegan would inherit the immense power and leadership of the Silvermoon Pack.

As he read on, the journal described the rituals, the traditions, the secrets that governed the werewolf world. He learned about the transformation, the excruciating pain, the uncontrollable rage, the unleashing of primal instincts. He learned about the power that lay dormant within him, a power that could both save and destroy. His hands trembled as he turned the final page, the weight of his destiny settling upon him, a heavy cloak of responsibility that promised both exhilarating power and terrifying danger. He was no longer just Damian Miller, a quiet boy from Oakhaven. He was something more, something ancient, something powerful, and something utterly terrifying. The blood moon, a malevolent eye in the night sky, pulsed with a menacing energy, a silent countdown to the night that would forever change his life. The peaceful life he'd always known was over; the fight for his birthright and the survival of his people had begun.

The journal's brittle pages felt like parchment under his trembling fingers, the faded ink a ghostly echo of lives lived and lost. He traced the elegant script with his fingertip, each word a revelation, each sentence a seismic shift in his understanding of himself and the world around him. The truth, laid bare in this ancient text, was both exhilarating and terrifying. He, Damian Miller, the ordinary boy from Oakhaven, was anything but ordinary. He was the next Alpha, the leader of the Silvermoon Pack, a lineage of werewolves stretching back centuries.

The weight of this knowledge settled upon him like a physical burden, crushing the breath from his lungs. He reread passages, his eyes scanning the lines again and again, seeking confirmation, searching for some flaw in the narrative, some detail that would disprove the impossible truth. But the words remained, stark and undeniable, etched in the fading ink like a curse or a prophecy.

He learned of the ancient rituals, the sacred ceremonies that marked the transition into the Alpha's mantle. He read of the transformation, a harrowing ordeal that promised agonizing pain, uncontrollable rage, and a complete surrender to the primal instincts buried deep within his soul. He learned of the power, an unimaginable strength that flowed in his veins, a power that could both heal and destroy, a force of nature capable of shaping destinies.

His initial reaction was one of sheer disbelief, a denial so profound it was almost a defense mechanism. It couldn't be true. He was just Damian, the quiet boy who loved the smell of woodsmoke and freshly baked bread, the boy who spent his days laughing with his friends, the boy who'd never known anything beyond the simple comforts of the Miller's farmhouse. This world of werewolves, of ancient prophecies and ruthless rivals, felt like a nightmare ripped from the pages of the gothic novels he devoured.

Yet, the evidence was irrefutable. The journal spoke of family crests, of ancestral lands, of rituals passed down through generations. It detailed the history of the Silvermoon Pack, its triumphs and its tragedies, its struggles against the darkness that perpetually threatened to consume it. The details were too specific, too intricate to be mere fabrication. It was history, a history that inextricably linked him to a lineage he'd never known existed.

A wave of nausea washed over him. He clutched the journal to his chest, his heart hammering a frantic rhythm against his ribs. The blood moon, still visible through his window, seemed to pulse with a malevolent energy, casting an eerie crimson glow across his room. It was as if the moon itself was a silent witness to his revelation, a spectral observer of his descent into this supernatural world.

He felt a strange mixture of awe and terror. Awe at the potential power, at the strength and influence that lay dormant within him, waiting to be unleashed. Terror at the responsibility, the immense weight of leadership that now rested on his young shoulders. He was no longer a teenager worrying about school and friends; he was a future Alpha, a leader of his pack, responsible for the safety and well-being of an entire community.

His internal conflict was fierce. A part of him longed to reject it all, to shut the journal, to return to the comfortable simplicity of his previous existence. The life he'd known, with its predictability and safety, suddenly seemed impossibly distant, a cherished memory fading into the shadow of his new reality.

But another part of him, a deeper, more primal part, felt a strange pull towards this newly revealed heritage. He felt a kinship with the ancient words, a connection to the lineage detailed in the faded ink. He sensed a stirring within him, a powerful energy that resonated with the moon's crimson glow, a nascent power that promised both exhilaration and danger.

The journal spoke of his uncle, Keegan, the leader of the rival Shadowfang Pack. Keegan, a man described as ruthless, ambitious, and utterly without conscience, was the biggest threat. The details painted a chilling portrait of a man driven by a thirst for power, a man who would stop at nothing to claim the Alpha's mantle, even if it meant eliminating his own nephew. The thought of facing Keegan, of engaging in a battle for the leadership of the werewolf clans, sent a shiver down his spine. The weight of this confrontation, the understanding that his survival was critical to the future of the Silvermoon Pack, added another layer to the turmoil brewing within him.

The journal mentioned the impending transformation, the full moon's arrival, and the critical timeframe. If he were to die before the blood moon's peak, Keegan would inherit the leadership of the Silvermoon Pack. The weight of this knowledge was crushing. This was not merely a battle for power; it was a fight for survival, for the future of his entire lineage, his clan, and his people.

He spent the rest of the night poring over the journal, absorbing every detail, every warning, every cryptic message. The words painted a picture of a world far more complex and dangerous than he could have ever imagined. It was a world where ancient rivalries and supernatural powers clashed, a world of shadows and secrets, of loyalty and betrayal. It was a world that he was now a part of, a world that demanded his courage, his strength, and his unwavering resolve. The blood moon continued to cast its spectral glow, a silent observer of his awakening, a stark reminder of the incredible destiny that awaited him. He closed the journal, the weight of its contents still settling upon him, as a new dawn broke, ushering in a new chapter of his life—a chapter filled with both unimaginable power and terrifying uncertainty. The fight for his birthright had begun. And Damian Miller, the ordinary boy, was gone, replaced by a warrior, an Alpha, a werewolf, ready to face the challenges of his destiny. The future held both immense power and the threat of annihilation, and only time would tell which path he would ultimately walk.

A low growl rumbled in Damian's chest, a sound so primal, so alien, it sent a jolt of pure terror through him. He was sitting at his desk, rereading a particularly gruesome passage about werewolf battles from his great-great-grandfather's journal, when it hit him – a wave of heat, a tightening in his muscles, an overwhelming urge to...tear something apart. His hands, usually steady, trembled as claws, long and sharp, extended from his fingertips. Panic seized him; he slammed the journal shut, his heart hammering against his ribs like a trapped bird.

The transformation wasn't complete, not yet. It was a fleeting glimpse, a terrifying preview of what was to come, but enough to leave him breathless and shaken. He looked down at his hands, watching in horrified fascination as the claws retracted, the transformation receding as quickly as it had begun. The heat subsided, leaving behind a lingering tremor in his limbs and a chilling awareness of the raw power simmering beneath his skin. It was exhilarating, terrifying, and utterly overwhelming.

Over the next few days, the involuntary shifts became more frequent, more intense. They were triggered by stress, by fear, even by the sudden scent of blood – a particularly unnerving experience when he accidentally cut himself while slicing bread.

Each episode left him drained, exhausted, but also strangely invigorated, as if a sleeping giant within him was slowly awakening.

He started to notice other changes, subtle at first, then increasingly pronounced. His senses heightened dramatically. Sounds that were once muted became crystal clear; distant conversations, the rustling of leaves, the soft scuttling of insects - all became audible with unnerving clarity. His sense of smell was similarly amplified, able to detect the subtle nuances of scents that humans never registered, like the earthy musk of the forest floor or the faint metallic tang of blood in the air, even when the source was miles away.

One evening, while walking through the woods near his home, he encountered a figure emerging from the shadows. The figure was tall and imposing, radiating an almost palpable aura of power. He had seen the symbol on the crest that appeared in the ancient journal; a Silvermoon crest on the leather-bound jacket. He realized, with a wave of both excitement and trepidation, that he was in the presence of another werewolf.

The werewolf, a woman with eyes like molten silver and hair the color of a midnight sky, introduced herself as Lyra. She was one of the Silvermoon Pack's elders, a seasoned warrior who had been watching Damian from afar. Lyra confirmed his heritage and explained the urgency of his training. The blood moon was fast approaching; his transformation was imminent, and he was woefully unprepared.

Lyra took him to a hidden clearing deep within the woods – the Silvermoon Pack's secret meeting place. The clearing was bathed in the ethereal glow of the moon, its ancient trees their silent sentinels. He met other members of the pack: hardened veterans, young pups barely beginning their transformations, and wise elders who had lived for centuries. They were a diverse group, united by their heritage and the strength of their pack.

The meetings were filled with whispered discussions, cryptic warnings, and shared stories of past battles against their rivals, the Shadowfang Pack. He learned about the history of the Silvermoon Pack, about its ancient alliances and bitter betrayals, its triumphs and tragedies. He learned of the intricate social dynamics within the pack, the hierarchies, the allegiances, and the simmering resentments that threatened to tear them apart from within.

Damian discovered that the werewolf world was far more complex than he had ever imagined. It wasn't simply a battle between good and evil; it was a tangled web of ambition, jealousy, and power struggles, where even long-standing alliances could unravel at any moment. The Shadowfang Pack, led by his ruthless uncle Keegan, was a constant threat, their presence felt even in the secluded meeting place. Their reputation preceded them: tales of brutal violence, ruthless power grabs, and cold-blooded betrayals filled the conversations in hushed tones.

The training was grueling. Lyra pushed Damian to his physical and mental limits, teaching him to harness his newfound abilities, to control his transformations, and to fight with the ferocity and precision of a seasoned warrior. He learned to control the raw power surging through his veins, to channel his rage into strength, and to use his enhanced senses to anticipate his opponent's moves. He learned to utilize his enhanced senses to anticipate threats, his speed to evade attacks, his strength to overcome obstacles. He trained alongside the other young pups, forging bonds of loyalty and friendship amidst the rigor of their training. The training also included lessons in pack history, ancient rituals, and the complex social structure of werewolf society.

One night, during a training exercise, a group of Shadowfang scouts infiltrated the clearing, intent on capturing Damian. A fierce battle ensued, a brutal clash of supernatural powers, claws and teeth clashing in a whirlwind of fur and moonlight. Damian, despite his limited experience, fought with a ferociousness that surprised even Lyra. The training he had undergone showed results; his instincts were sharpened, his movements fluid, his power undeniable. The scouts were repelled, but not without leaving their mark. One of the elders was injured, a reminder of the ever-present danger looming over the Silvermoon Pack.

The incident underscored the growing threat posed by Keegan and the Shadowfang Pack. The attack was a clear indication of Keegan's intent: he was not merely seeking to usurp the Alpha's position; he was attempting to eradicate the Silvermoon Pack altogether. The blood moon loomed closer, the time frame narrowing. Damian's transformation was fast approaching, the stakes were high, and his future uncertain. The weight of his destiny, the burden of leadership, pressed down on him, intensifying the urgency of his training and his preparation for the inevitable confrontation with his uncle.

The clandestine meetings continued. He learned more about the ancient prophecies that foretold his arrival and the consequences of his failure. He learned of rituals designed to strengthen his bond with the pack and amplify his powers. He also learned about the delicate balance of power that maintained order among the various werewolf packs and the consequences of disrupting that balance. The atmosphere was thick with anticipation, fear, and the palpable presence of the supernatural. The forest itself seemed to hold its breath, awaiting the arrival of the blood moon. The air itself hummed with the energy generated by the moon's presence, an ever-present reminder of the impending transformation, and Damian felt this energy more deeply than most, as though the moon itself were a mirror reflecting his own growing power. As the blood moon edged closer, so too did the danger, the intensity of the conflict ratcheting up with each passing day. He knew, with chilling certainty, that the fight for his birthright, and the survival of the Silvermoon Pack, was about to begin in earnest.

Lyra, her silver eyes gleaming in the moonlight, led Damian to a secluded waterfall cascading into a crystal-clear pool. The air here hummed with a different kind of energy, a raw, untamed power that resonated with the burgeoning strength within him. "This," she said, her voice a low, melodious purr, "is where we begin."

The training was unlike anything Damian had ever experienced. It wasn't simply about physical combat, though that formed a significant part of it. Lyra focused on controlling his transformations, teaching him to shift at will, to regulate the surge of power that threatened to overwhelm him. The initial attempts were disastrous. One moment he'd be a human, the next a raging beast, claws extended, teeth bared, barely able to comprehend his own actions. He lashed out, inadvertently shattering several ancient trees before Lyra, with a speed that defied his comprehension, restrained him. The sheer power of her grip, the force of her will, was breathtaking.

"Control, Damian," she growled, her voice low and intense, "Control is the key. Your power is immense, but without control, it's a weapon you cannot wield."

Days turned into weeks, filled with rigorous exercises designed to hone his control. He learned to meditate, to focus his mind, to quiet the primal urges that threatened to consume him. He spent hours practicing his shifts, transitioning smoothly from human to werewolf and back, each transformation becoming progressively smoother, more precise, less violent. The initial, chaotic shifts were replaced by controlled transitions, the transformation process becoming almost balletic in its elegance. Lyra would often push him to his limit, placing him in scenarios designed to test his self-control – confronting him with the scents of blood, forcing him into claustrophobic situations designed to test his emotional stability.

Lyra wasn't merely teaching him physical control; she was teaching him emotional control, showing him how to manage his rage, his fear, his anxieties. She explained how his emotions fueled his transformations, how uncontrolled emotions could lead to unpredictable and dangerous shifts. She taught him to channel his rage into focused strength, transforming his fear into heightened awareness, using his anxieties as fuel for his determination. She taught him to control his breath, to calm his heart rate, to find a quiet center within the storm raging within him. This inner quiet, she explained, was the key to harnessing his full power.

Physical training was equally intense. She taught him hand-to-hand combat, sparring with him relentlessly, her movements fluid and lethal. Her blows were swift, precise, leaving him bruised and breathless, but always pushing him further, always pushing him to exceed his own expectations. He learned to fight using his claws, his teeth, his enhanced strength and speed, to use the environment to his advantage. He learned to use the terrain, the trees, the rocks, as weapons, using the cover of darkness to his advantage, moving with a speed and grace that was both terrifying and captivating.

Lyra's training incorporated elements of strategy and tactics. She taught him to read his opponents, to anticipate their moves, to exploit their weaknesses. She spoke of the importance of discipline, of precision, of strategic thinking, of always planning for every possible scenario. She drilled him in tactics, teaching him how to fight as a member of a pack, how to work in coordination with others, utilizing the strength of the pack to overwhelm and defeat opponents. He studied the ancient tactics of the Silvermoon Pack, learning from their past victories and defeats, understanding how to utilize the environment, the cover of darkness and the strength of the pack to their advantage.

Beyond the physical and strategic aspects, Lyra delved into the history of the Silvermoon Pack, its rituals, and its ancient prophecies. She recounted tales of legendary werewolves, of epic battles fought and won, of sacrifices made and legacies forged. She showed him ancient scrolls detailing the pack's history, revealing the stories of its founders, its struggles for survival, its triumphs and its tragedies. She spoke of the blood moon prophecy, clarifying the ancient scriptures, expanding his understanding of its implications, and emphasizing the necessity of his role in fulfilling this prophecy.

One evening, as the blood moon hung heavy in the sky, casting an eerie red glow over the forest, Lyra took Damian to a sacred grove. There, amidst the ancient trees, she initiated him into the Silvermoon Pack's ancient rituals. The rituals were designed to strengthen his connection with the pack, to enhance his innate abilities, and to prepare him for the challenges that lay ahead. They invoked the spirits of his ancestors, seeking their guidance and protection. They involved chanting ancient incantations, offering prayers, and performing ancient dances to invoke the power of the moon and the earth. The rituals were physically and emotionally draining, but they forged a deep bond between Damian and the spirits of the pack, his ancestors and the land.

Through it all, Lyra's guidance was unwavering. She pushed him hard, but she was also patient and understanding. She saw his struggles, his doubts, his fears, and she met them with compassion and wisdom. Their relationship evolved from mentor and student to something deeper, a bond of mutual respect and trust. She became more than just a teacher; she became a friend, a confidante, a source of strength in a world that was increasingly dangerous and unpredictable. He learned to trust her implicitly, relying on her wisdom and guidance to navigate the complex world he had so unexpectedly entered.

As the blood moon approached, the training intensified. The urgency of the situation was palpable, the tension ratcheting up with each passing day. Lyra prepared Damian for the inevitable confrontation with his uncle, Keegan, and the Shadowfang Pack. She taught him not just how to fight, but how to lead, how to inspire, how to unite the pack in the face of overwhelming odds. She instilled in him the importance of loyalty, bravery, and the strength that only unity could bring.

The final days of training were brutal, but they forged within Damian a strength, a confidence, that he never knew he possessed. He stood ready, no longer the frightened young man who had stumbled upon his heritage, but a seasoned warrior, ready to face whatever challenges lay ahead, prepared to fight for his birthright and the survival of his pack, under the watchful eye, and guidance, of his powerful mentor. The bond they formed, forged in the crucible of intense training and shared danger, would prove invaluable as he faced the dark forces that threatened to consume him and his pack. The blood moon was near, and Damian, armed with his newfound skills and the unwavering support of his mentor, was finally ready.

The air crackled with anticipation, the scent of pine and damp earth heavy with the impending storm. Lyra, her silver eyes reflecting the growing crimson glow of the blood moon, traced the lines of an ancient map etched onto a weathered piece of bark. "Keegan's reach is far greater than you realize, Damian," she murmured, her voice barely above a whisper. "He's not just a brute; he's a strategist, a manipulator. He's spent years weaving a web of deceit, gathering allies, and consolidating his power."

She pointed to a cluster of darkened symbols on the map, each representing a territory under Keegan's control. "These are the remnants of smaller packs, absorbed into the Shadowfang pack, their members either assimilated or... eliminated. He uses charm and intimidation in equal measure, promising power and protection to those too weak to resist, crushing those who dare to defy him."

A shiver ran down Damian's spine. He'd always viewed Keegan as a distant, shadowy figure, a malevolent uncle mentioned in hushed whispers. But now, seeing the scope of his uncle's influence laid out before him, the full extent of his cruelty became chillingly clear.

Lyra's words painted a grim picture: a merciless dictator who consolidated power through treachery and brutal force, leaving a trail of broken packs and silenced dissenters in his wake.

Lyra continued, her voice taking on a steely edge. "He's not merely ambitious; he's consumed by a thirst for dominance. He craves the power bestowed by the blood moon, the power to control the entire werewolf population, not just the Shadowfang pack." She paused, her gaze piercing. "He believes he is destined to rule, that the prophecy foretold his reign. He sees you as an obstacle, a threat to his ambitions. He won't hesitate to eliminate you, and anyone who stands in his way."

Damian recalled the few times he'd encountered Keegan as a child, fleeting glimpses of a cold, calculating man, whose smile never reached his eyes. Those memories, once vague and unimportant, now took on a sinister significance. He remembered the chilling emptiness in his uncle's gaze, the unnerving stillness of his movements. He understood now that those weren't just quirks of personality; they were the hallmarks of a man who had lived in the shadows, a man who knew the art of manipulation and deception.

Lyra described several instances that illustrated Keegan's ruthlessness. There was the tale of the Whisperwind Pack, once a proud and independent group, now utterly eradicated. Keegan, under the guise of an alliance, had infiltrated their ranks, poisoning their leadership, turning members against each other before swiftly eliminating them all, seizing their territory and resources for himself. Then there was the story of the Nightshade Clan, a powerful coven of witches, manipulated by Keegan into betraying their allegiance to the Silvermoon Pack, a betrayal that cost the Silvermoon Pack dearly. And finally, there was the chilling account of the Bloodstone tribe, a fierce community of shapeshifters, annihilated by Keegan in an act of calculated savagery.

Each story was a chilling testament to Keegan's ambition and cruelty. Lyra emphasized the careful planning that underlay Keegan's actions, highlighting his strategic acumen, his capacity for manipulation, his skill at leveraging fear and uncertainty to achieve his goals. He didn't simply conquer; he manipulated, he infiltrated, he sowed discord and then reaped the rewards, his methods as cold and calculating as the winter winds. He was a master strategist, a puppeteer pulling the strings of the werewolf world, his actions always calculated, designed to serve his greater, ruthless agenda.

Lyra's narrative painted a stark contrast between Keegan's insidious tactics and the Silvermoon Pack's traditional values of honor, loyalty, and mutual respect. The Silvermoon Pack had always strived for peaceful coexistence, resolving conflicts through diplomacy and negotiation, preferring understanding and alliance to conquest and domination. This philosophy, however noble, had left them vulnerable to Keegan's cunning maneuvers. He exploited their trust, their inherent goodness, turning their virtues against them.

The implications of Keegan's actions extended far beyond the loss of lives and territories. His influence was slowly but surely altering the balance of power within the werewolf world, threatening to usher in an era of darkness and tyranny. Lyra spoke of alliances forged, broken, and reforged, each maneuver a testament to Keegan's relentless pursuit of power. He had mastered the art of manipulation, turning werewolves against each other, creating division and chaos, weakening the very fabric of the werewolf society, making it easier for his shadow to engulf it entirely.

Lyra then shifted the focus to the prophecy itself, revealing the deeper connection between the blood moon and Keegan's ambitions. The prophecy didn't just speak of a powerful werewolf arising during the blood moon; it also spoke of a shadow, a dark force that threatened to consume the werewolf world. Lyra argued that Keegan, with his insatiable thirst for power and his ruthless tactics, was the very embodiment of that shadow. His actions were a fulfillment of the prophecy's darker implications, not the intended heroic outcome.

"The prophecy speaks of balance, Damian," Lyra explained, her voice firm. "A balance between light and shadow, between power and responsibility. Keegan seeks only power, disregarding the responsibility that comes with it. He's twisting the prophecy to suit his own dark designs, using it as a justification for his tyranny."

The weight of responsibility settled heavily on Damian's shoulders. He was no longer just fighting for his own survival, but for the survival of his pack, his community, and the entire werewolf world. The threat wasn't just Keegan's physical strength, but his cunning, his influence, and the insidious shadow he cast over everything. The training had prepared him physically, but nothing could fully prepare him for the psychological warfare he was about to face. He had to not only be strong, but also shrewd, capable of outwitting his uncle's cunning and countering his manipulations. He had to understand the nuances of his uncle's game and anticipate his moves, becoming not just a warrior, but a strategist, matching wits with the most cunning and ruthless werewolf in existence.

The night deepened, the blood moon casting an increasingly menacing red glow over the forest. Lyra pulled out a small, intricately carved wooden box. Inside, nestled on a bed of crimson velvet, lay a silver amulet – the Silvermoon crest, symbol of the pack's leadership, its ancient power now resting in Damian's hands.

"This," Lyra said, her voice solemn, "is the symbol of your legacy, Damian. It is more than just a symbol; it's a conduit, a connection to the power of the Silvermoon Pack, to your ancestors. Wear it with pride, and wear it with strength. You are now not just a werewolf; you are a leader."

Damian took the amulet, the cool silver against his skin sending a wave of power through him. The responsibility weighed heavily on him, the enormity of the task before him daunting. He was facing not just a physical battle, but a struggle against the very essence of darkness that had taken root within his own family. The training had been grueling, but this, the knowledge of Keegan's ambition and the looming threat of his shadow, was the true test. He was ready, yet he still felt a tremble of apprehension deep within, a mix of fear and determination that settled in his soul like the chilling night wind. The blood moon prophecy had become terrifyingly real, and his fate, the fate of the Silvermoon Pack, rested on his shoulders. The fight for the future had begun.

Chapter 2:
Training and Betrayal

The air thinned, the scent of pine replaced by the sharp tang of sweat and exertion. Lyra, her silver eyes gleaming with an intensity that matched the blood moon's crimson glow, surveyed Damian. Weeks blurred into a relentless cycle of training, each day pushing him to his physical and mental limits. The forest became his arena, its trees his sparring partners, its shadows his instructors. Lyra, a whirlwind of motion and precise instruction, guided him through a rigorous regimen designed to hone his innate werewolf abilities.

First came the control of the shift. The initial transformations were chaotic, painful eruptions of primal energy. Damian thrashed, limbs contorting, muscles straining, his senses overwhelmed by a torrent of raw power. He felt like a storm raging within a cage, desperate to break free. Lyra, however, was relentless, forcing him to focus, to channel the energy, to find the calm eye within the tempest. She guided him through meditation techniques, teaching him to breathe in harmony with the moon's rhythm, to connect with the ancient pulse of the werewolf essence that flowed within him. Slowly, painstakingly, he learned to regulate the transformation, to shift at will, to control the ferocity of his beast form.

Next came the honing of his senses. Lyra blindfolded him, forcing him to rely on his enhanced hearing and smell. He learned to distinguish the rustle of a leaf from the tread of a foot, the subtle scent of fear from the sharp tang of blood. He could smell the fear in a rabbit a hundred yards away, and he could hear the beating of a hummingbird's wings from across the clearing. She led him through complex obstacle courses in total darkness, his heightened senses his only guide. He navigated treacherous terrain, leaping over ravines, scaling cliffs, his movements fluid and precise, guided by the whispers of the night.

Then came the combat training. Lyra was a formidable opponent, a blur of motion, her strikes precise and deadly. She taught him the ancient fighting techniques of the Silvermoon Pack, a style that blended raw power with elegant grace, agility with brute force. She sparred with him relentlessly, pushing him past his breaking point, forcing him to adapt, to learn, to evolve. His body screamed in protest, his muscles aching, his bones bruised, but he persevered, driven by a fierce determination to master his abilities. Each fall, each defeat, only fueled his resolve, strengthening his body and sharpening his mind.

He learned to fight with the ferocity of a wolf, but with the calculated precision of a warrior. He learned to read his opponent's movements, to anticipate their attacks, to exploit their weaknesses. He practiced wielding various weapons, learning the deadly arts of both hand-to-hand combat and weaponry. He learned to use his fangs and claws to deadly effect, his bite as swift and venomous as a viper's strike. He learned to utilize the terrain to his advantage, using the shadows as camouflage and the trees as cover. He trained to fight not just to kill, but to subdue, to protect, to uphold the principles of the Silvermoon Pack despite the grim reality of the threat they faced.

He practiced strategies, tactics, planning escapes and ambush maneuvers, all with a constant focus on precision and efficiency. He learned to think like a wolf, to rely on his instincts, yet to maintain the rationality that set him apart from a mindless beast. The line between man and wolf blurred, becoming something new, something stronger. He became a blend of two worlds. He learned to trust his instincts, to follow the path of the hunter, to feel the thrill of the chase, to taste the sweet reward of victory. Yet, he also honed his analytical skills, learning to assess situations, strategize plans, and anticipate his enemy's moves.

The culmination of his training was a final test—a trial by combat against Lyra herself. The forest floor trembled under their clashing forms, trees splintering as their blows landed with devastating force. Lyra fought with the skill of a seasoned warrior, her movements as fluid as water, her strikes as precise as lightning. Damian, however, matched her every move, his newfound strength and agility allowing him to withstand her onslaught. Their battle was a dance of death, a furious ballet of power and skill, a testament to the grueling training he had endured.

Finally, exhausted but triumphant, he emerged victorious, not by brute force, but by strategy and skill. He disarmed her, not with a violent move, but with a controlled maneuver that reflected both power and grace. Lyra, satisfied, nodded, her eyes filled with a mixture of pride and caution. The training was complete, but the true test lay ahead. He stood there, breathless but resolute. The training had instilled not just physical prowess but mental fortitude, a sharpening of his senses and an understanding of the nuances of combat that would prove essential against Keegan. He had learned to harness the power within, but the true challenge was yet to come.

The triumph was short-lived. The celebration of his hard-won victory was abruptly cut short by a chilling betrayal. While he celebrated his accomplishment, a figure slipped through the shadows, a viper in human form, someone he had grown to trust. This person, a member of the Silvermoon Pack who had pledged his allegiance and helped with his training, revealed their true colors. The betrayal struck like a poisoned dagger. The news was shocking—they were working with Keegan, providing vital information that detailed Damian's training, his strengths, his weaknesses, and the very nature of the plan to confront his uncle.

The information leaked wasn't merely details about his physical prowess; it also betrayed the strategic plans Lyra and Damian had meticulously developed over weeks. The traitor had provided a map of their intended approach, the timing of their movements, and the critical points in their plan that could be exploited. Damian felt a chilling wave of despair wash over him. The trust he had placed in this individual, the bond he had felt, was shattered, replaced by a bitter taste of betrayal. He had overcome physical challenges, honed his skills, but the psychological blow was perhaps even more devastating.

The betrayal was not simply a matter of lost tactical advantage. It went deeper, striking at the very heart of the Silvermoon Pack, eroding the foundation of loyalty and trust that held it together. The act revealed a fissure within the pack, a hidden weakness that Keegan could exploit. It shattered the sense of unity that was essential to their survival against the overwhelming threat of Keegan's growing empire. Damian felt a surge of anger, a burning desire for revenge, but he knew that he couldn't afford to let his emotions cloud his judgment.

He stood alone in the shadows, the weight of betrayal pressing down on him. The hard-won strength gained through training now felt inadequate against this new, insidious threat. The battle wasn't merely physical; it was psychological, a war of wits, a dance of deception, and the betrayal exposed a vulnerability that far exceeded anything he'd faced in his physical training. The blood moon, once a symbol of hope and power, now seemed to mock him with its crimson glow, a reminder of the darkness that lurked within his own family and the treacherous path that lay ahead. The weight of the pack's fate rested heavily on his shoulders, heavier than any weapon he could wield. His journey to confront Keegan had become more intricate and dangerous than he could have ever imagined. The game of strategy had begun, a game where the stakes were not just his life, but the future of the Silvermoon Pack.

The sting of betrayal lingered, a bitter aftertaste to the victory he'd so hard-earned. Lyra, her face etched with grim determination, placed a comforting hand on his shoulder. "We need to understand *why*," she said, her voice low and serious. "This wasn't a random act. It was calculated, precise. It speaks to a deeper conspiracy."

Damian nodded, the anger simmering beneath the surface. His mind raced, replaying the events of the past few weeks, searching for clues, for anything that might shed light on the traitor's motives. The revelation had shaken him to his core, not just because of the strategic setback, but because the betrayal had come from within the pack, from someone he'd considered an ally. The trust, once unshakeable, was now shattered, leaving him vulnerable and uncertain.

Lyra led him to the pack's archives, a dimly lit chamber filled with ancient scrolls, dusty tomes, and weathered maps. The air hung heavy with the scent of aged parchment and forgotten secrets. She explained that the Silvermoon Pack's history was a tapestry woven with threads of loyalty, betrayal, and internecine conflict. Generations of werewolves had fought for power, their struggles echoing through the ages.

They began their search, sifting through centuries of records, unraveling the tangled threads of family history. Damian learned about his great-grandfather, a revered leader whose reign had been marked by both glory and bloodshed. He discovered a hidden feud that had fractured the pack, a struggle for dominance that had almost brought about its downfall. He learned about secret alliances, clandestine meetings, and hidden agendas that had shaped the pack's destiny. The stories were a stark reminder that the current conflict with Keegan was not an isolated incident but a continuation of a long-standing struggle for power.

One particular scroll caught their attention, detailing a prophecy foretelling a great upheaval within the pack, a betrayal that would threaten its very existence. The prophecy spoke of a wolf marked by destiny, a leader who would rise to overcome the darkness, but also of a hidden enemy, a traitor within the pack who would aid the opposing forces. The details were vague, shrouded in cryptic language and symbolic imagery, but the chilling parallels to their current situation were undeniable.

As they delved deeper into the archives, they unearthed a hidden compartment containing a collection of personal letters written by Damian's grandfather. The letters revealed a complex family drama, a story of love, loss, and bitter rivalry between two brothers, Damian's grandfather and Keegan's father. The letters chronicled a bitter power struggle that had split the pack, a conflict fuelled by ambition and resentment.

The letters painted a picture of Keegan's father as a ruthless and ambitious individual who craved power and dominance. He had challenged Damian's grandfather for leadership, creating a deep rift that had fractured the family. The rivalry between the two brothers had spilled over into the next generation, fueling the current conflict between Damian and Keegan. The past, it seemed, cast a long shadow, shaping the present and determining the course of the future.

Damian discovered that the feud had a deeper root than a mere power struggle. It was intertwined with a long-forgotten feud between two werewolf clans, one aligned with his grandfather and the other with Keegan's father. This ancient feud dated back centuries, its origins lost in the mists of time, yet its consequences continued to reverberate through the generations. The rivalry was not just between two brothers; it was a continuation of a generational conflict between clans, each vying for supremacy.

The letters also revealed the existence of a sacred artifact, a powerful amulet passed down through generations, said to hold the key to unlocking the ancient power of the werewolf lineage. The amulet had been lost long ago, swallowed by the passage of time, but its presence served as a constant reminder of the power struggles and the significance of their legacy. The quest for this amulet, lost within the tumultuous events of the past, could be the key to understanding the origins of the conflict. The pursuit of this legendary amulet became a pivotal element in their quest to unravel the family secrets and defeat Keegan.

As Damian pieced together the fragments of his family history, he realized that his conflict with Keegan was not just about power, but also about heritage, about the legacy of his ancestors. He was fighting not only for his own survival but also for the survival of his clan, for the preservation of their history and traditions. This realization infused him with a newfound resolve, a determination to confront his uncle and settle the ancient score once and for all.

The weight of history, of generations of conflict, rested heavily on his shoulders. He felt the burden of his ancestors, their hopes, their dreams, their struggles. He understood that his fight wasn't just against Keegan, but against the very shadows of his family's past. The past was not merely a chronicle of events; it was a living entity, influencing the present, shaping the destiny of the Silvermoon Pack.

His search revealed another shocking truth. The traitor, the one who had betrayed their trust, was not merely a pawn in Keegan's game but a descendant of the rival clan, a descendant who had been manipulated and manipulated for generations to fuel the family feud, a puppet playing out a role in a centuries-old drama. This realization added another layer of complexity to the situation, highlighting the long-reaching and insidious nature of the conflict. The traitor's actions were not driven by personal greed but by a deep-seated loyalty to an ancient blood feud.

The investigation wasn't merely a historical exercise; it was a desperate race against time. Each clue uncovered brought them closer to understanding Keegan's strategy, his weaknesses, his ultimate goal. It also revealed how deeply rooted the deception was, how many within the Silvermoon Pack had been complicit, either knowingly or unknowingly. The true extent of Keegan's network was still unknown. The lines of loyalty were blurred, making it nearly impossible to identify true allies from deceitful spies.

The weight of this discovery pressed down on Damian, the revelation intensifying the challenge ahead. It wasn't enough to defeat Keegan physically; he had to dismantle the intricate network of deceit and manipulation that Keegan had woven throughout the generations. He had to sever the threads that bound the pack to Keegan's father's legacy of manipulation. This required more than just physical strength or tactical brilliance; it required unmasking the truth and exposing the intricate web of deceit that threatened to destroy the Silvermoon Pack from within.

The moonlight streamed through the high, arched windows of the archive, casting long shadows across the dusty floor. Lyra stood beside him, her eyes reflecting the intensity of the situation. They had uncovered the secrets, but the journey was far from over. The path ahead was fraught with danger, but armed with the knowledge of the past, they were ready to face the future. The fight for the Silvermoon Pack's survival had become a battle not only against a ruthless uncle but against a legacy of deceit and betrayal that had spanned generations. The true test of Damian's strength, his leadership, and his resolve lay ahead. The game was far from over; the fight for the future of the Silvermoon Pack was just beginning.

The air crackled with anticipation, the scent of pine and damp earth mingling with the sharp, metallic tang of blood. Damian stood poised, muscles coiled like springs, his senses heightened to the extreme. Before him, a clearing in the Whispering Woods was bathed in the ethereal glow of the late afternoon sun, the trees forming a silent, watchful audience. He'd tracked Keegan's forces for days, following a trail of broken branches and disturbed earth, each clue fueling his burning resolve. This was it – his first true test, his baptism of fire.

He wasn't alone. Lyra, her face a mask of grim determination, stood at his side, her silver claws glinting ominously in the dappled light. Beside her, a hulking figure, Kael, one of the few remaining loyal members of the Silvermoon Pack, shifted restlessly, his powerful muscles rippling beneath his thick fur. Kael, a seasoned warrior, his experience a stark contrast to Damian's nascent skills, provided a reassuring presence, a bulwark against the uncertainty of the upcoming battle.

The woods erupted into a cacophony of snarls and growls. From the shadows emerged Keegan's vanguard – a dozen werewolves, their eyes burning with a predatory gleam, their forms taut with aggression. They were a formidable force, each one a veteran of countless battles, their movements fluid and deadly. At their head stood a towering figure, his frame even larger than Kael's, his fur the color of midnight, his eyes blazing with icy fury. This was Roric, Keegan's most trusted lieutenant, a werewolf whose reputation for brutality preceded him.

Roric let out a deafening roar, a challenge that echoed through the woods, shaking the very leaves from the trees. "Damian," he snarled, his voice thick with venom, "Your reign of defiance ends here."

The battle began with a savage fury. Damian launched himself forward, his movements a blur of motion, his claws tearing through the air, leaving trails of crimson in their wake. His training with Lyra had honed his instincts, his reflexes sharpened to a razor's edge. He moved with a primal grace, a deadly ballet of teeth and claws, each strike precise and devastating.

He engaged Roric first, a clash of titans, a brutal exchange of blows. Roric was a formidable opponent, his strength and experience a match for Damian's youthful ferocity. Their fight was a whirlwind of snarls and growls, a brutal dance of destruction, the air thick with the stench of sweat and blood. Damian found himself struggling to match Roric's power, his own strength tested to its limits.

Lyra and Kael engaged the remaining werewolves, their combined skills a force to be reckoned with. Lyra, nimble and agile, weaved through the enemy ranks, her silver claws leaving deep gashes in their flesh. Kael, a brute force of nature, met each attack head-on, his powerful blows sending werewolves sprawling. The battle raged, a chaotic maelstrom of snarls and growls, teeth and claws, a desperate struggle for survival.

Damian found himself overwhelmed, momentarily knocked back by Roric's raw power. He felt the sting of defeat, the bitter taste of failure, a stark reminder of his relative inexperience. He stumbled, his breath ragged, his body aching, a wave of discouragement washing over him. He was about to fall, the darkness closing in, when he caught a glimpse of Lyra's determined gaze. Her silent encouragement, her unwavering belief in him, reignited his resolve.

He pushed past the pain, the fatigue, the doubt, digging deep into the well of his strength, his will hardening like steel. He rose to his feet, his eyes burning with a renewed ferocity. He had to win. He had to prove himself. He had to protect the pack.

He launched himself at Roric again, his attack sharper, more precise, fueled by a newfound determination. He used his agility to his advantage, dodging Roric's heavy blows, his movements fluid and unpredictable. He exploited an opening, delivering a swift, devastating blow that sent Roric reeling. The fight continued, a brutal dance of power and skill, until, with a final, desperate lunge, Damian managed to bring Roric down, pinning him to the ground.

The tide of battle shifted. With Roric incapacitated, the remaining werewolves lost their resolve. They scattered, retreating into the shadows, their howls of defeat echoing through the trees. Damian stood victorious, panting, bruised, but undefeated. His first major battle had been won, but at a cost. The lingering injury, a deep gash across his shoulder, served as a stark reminder of the brutality of the conflict, and the challenges that lay ahead.

Lyra and Kael approached, their faces etched with relief and pride. They had seen his potential, his strength, his resilience, the fire in his heart that refused to be extinguished. This battle was not just a victory in the present; it was a testament to Damian's potential, his capacity to lead, his strength of character. But even as the victory settled over them, a chilling realization dawned. This was just the beginning. Keegan's forces were far stronger, far more numerous than they had initially estimated. The war for the Silvermoon Pack was far from over, and the path ahead would be a treacherous one, full of trials and tribulations. The victory was sweet, but the taste of battle was ever present, the anticipation of the next conflict already brewing. The fight for survival continued, the echoes of this first encounter reverberating through the silent woods, a testament to the trials ahead. The battle had been won, but the war was just beginning.

The aftermath of the battle revealed more than just physical wounds. The clearing was a scene of devastation, a testament to the ferocity of the encounter. The scent of blood hung heavy in the air, a grim reminder of the price of victory. As Damian examined his wounds, Lyra carefully tended to the deep gash on his shoulder, her touch gentle yet firm. Kael, ever vigilant, stood guard, his senses alert for any sign of the retreating enemy.

The silence that followed the battle was punctuated only by the rustling of leaves and the chirping of crickets, a stark contrast to the recent cacophony of violence. Yet, the silence held a palpable tension, an unspoken acknowledgement of the precariousness of their situation. The victory had been hard-won, but it had also revealed the depth of the threat they faced. Keegan's forces were far more formidable than they had anticipated, their numbers and strength far exceeding their initial estimates.

Damian, despite his exhaustion and injuries, felt a surge of resolve. This victory, though costly, had forged his spirit, sharpening his instincts and hardening his resolve. He knew that the fight was far from over, that the battles ahead would be even more challenging. But he also knew that he was not alone. He had Lyra, Kael, and the remaining loyal members of the Silvermoon

Pack to fight alongside him. They would face the coming storms together, their unity a bulwark against the encroaching darkness.

The moon rose in the sky, casting its silvery light upon the ravaged clearing. The air grew colder, the shadows lengthening, hinting at the darkness that still loomed ahead. But as Damian looked at his companions, he found solace in their shared determination, a quiet strength that fueled his resolve. The battle had been won, but the war was far from over. The path ahead was fraught with danger, but they would face it together. The future of the Silvermoon Pack hung in the balance, and their fight had only just begun.

The embers of the fire crackled, casting flickering shadows on the faces gathered around it. The air, still thick with the scent of blood and pine, carried a new, chilling undercurrent – the whisper of betrayal. Damian, his shoulder throbbing with the reminder of his recent battle, felt a knot of unease tighten in his stomach. The victory over Roric and Keegan's vanguard had been hard-fought, but it had come at a cost, a cost that extended far beyond physical wounds. The jubilation of their survival had been short-lived, replaced by a growing sense of unease.

Lyra, her silver eyes sharp and observant, broke the silence. "We underestimated Keegan," she stated, her voice low and grave. "His forces are far greater than we initially thought. And there's something else... something I don't understand."

Kael, his massive frame hunched over the fire, grunted in agreement. "I've sensed it too, Lyra. A shift in the wind, a change in the pack's rhythm. Something feels... off."

Their unease wasn't unfounded. Whispers had begun to circulate within the Silvermoon Pack, insidious rumors of dissent, of werewolves wavering in their loyalty. Damian had dismissed them initially, attributing them to fear and uncertainty in the face of Keegan's threat. But as days bled into nights, the whispers grew louder, more insistent, solidifying into a chilling reality. The betrayal, it turned out, wasn't coming from Keegan's forces alone. It was festering from within.

One evening, as Damian was patrolling the perimeter of their hidden sanctuary, a lone figure emerged from the shadows. It was Elara, a young she-wolf, once considered one of Damian's closest allies. Her eyes, usually bright with mischief, now held a cold, calculating gleam.

"Damian," she said, her voice barely a breath, "I have information you need to hear. Information that will change everything."

Elara revealed a shocking truth: a conspiracy within the pack, a cabal of werewolves secretly pledging their allegiance to Keegan, plotting to overthrow Damian and deliver the Silvermoon Pack to their enemy. She named names, outlining a web of deceit that snaked through the very heart of their community. Among the betrayers were werewolves Damian had considered friends, warriors he had fought alongside, their shared experiences forged in the crucible of battle seeming to vanish in the face of treachery.

The revelation struck Damian like a physical blow. The weight of betrayal pressed down on him, heavier than any physical injury. The faces of those he had trusted swam before his eyes, their smiles and camaraderie now twisted into grotesque masks of deception. He felt a deep, gut-wrenching sense of loss, the shattered fragments of trust forming a painful mosaic of disillusionment.

His initial reaction was one of anger, a burning rage that threatened to consume him. He wanted to confront the traitors, to rip them apart limb from limb. But Lyra, ever the pragmatist, intervened, reminding him of the danger. A hasty confrontation would only solidify Keegan's advantage, scattering their already depleted forces.

Instead, they hatched a plan, a delicate game of cat and mouse, designed to expose the traitors without igniting a civil war. Elara, a willing participant in their scheme, provided invaluable information – the location of the cabal's secret meetings, their code words, their plans. This clandestine war, fought in whispers and shadows, demanded patience, a virtue that Damian was still learning to master.

The following days were spent in a tense dance of deception. Damian played the part of the unsuspecting leader, feigning ignorance of the conspiracy while subtly gathering intelligence, observing the shifting loyalties within the pack. His every move, every word, was measured, calculated, his actions carefully choreographed to avoid arousing suspicion.

He approached some of the suspected traitors with offers of peace and reconciliation, testing their loyalty. Some remained steadfast in their deception, their words honeyed but their eyes betraying a coldness that chills Damian to his very core. Others wavered, their allegiances shifting like sands under his watchful gaze, betraying moments of uncertainty and guilt in their demeanour. It was a harrowing experience, witnessing the fragility of trust, the ease with which loyalty could be eroded by treachery.

The discovery of the traitorous werewolves wasn't without consequences. Internal strife began to fracture the already fragile unity of the Silvermoon Pack. Arguments erupted, accusations flew, and old friendships were torn apart. The atmosphere became one of suspicion and mistrust, where every conversation held a hidden agenda and every shadow concealed a potential threat. This turmoil tested the resilience of Damian's leadership, challenging his ability to maintain order amidst the chaos. His strength wasn't just being tested in battles with external enemies; he was fighting a war within his own ranks.

The climax arrived during a clandestine meeting of the cabal. Damian, guided by Elara and aided by a small group of trusted allies, infiltrated the gathering, confronting the traitors in their lair. The ensuing confrontation was brutal, a clash of claw and fang, fuelled by years of shared history now twisted into bitter hatred. The fight was vicious, close-quarters combat in a dimly lit cave that seemed to amplify the cacophony of snarls and growls, the air thick with the metallic tang of blood.

Damian fought with a ferociousness born of betrayal and fury, his movements a blur of motion, his rage a weapon as sharp as his claws. He spared no one, his blows ruthless and precise, each strike aimed to disarm and incapacitate, not kill. He didn't want a civil war, but he wouldn't allow the traitors to destroy the pack from within. The battle was a maelstrom of fur and teeth, a struggle not just for survival, but for the very soul of the Silvermoon Pack.

After the brutal struggle, the traitors were subdued, their treachery exposed. But the victory felt hollow, tainted by the loss of camaraderie and the fracture within the pack. The internal wounds were as deep, and perhaps even more difficult to heal, than any physical injury inflicted by Keegan's forces. The unity Damian so desperately needed was shattered, its pieces scattered like broken shards of glass. The path ahead remained uncertain and dangerous, a path shrouded in the shadows of betrayal. The war wasn't just about facing Keegan; it was about rebuilding trust and healing the deep divisions within the Silvermoon Pack – a task as daunting as facing Keegan's army.

The air hung heavy with the scent of pine and damp earth, a stark contrast to the metallic tang of blood that had clung to them for days. The aftermath of the internal conflict had left its mark, not just on the physical landscape of their sanctuary but also on the souls of the Silvermoon Pack. The silence that followed the brutal confrontation was more unsettling than any howl of impending battle. Damian, his body aching, his spirit weary, watched Lyra tend to the injured, her movements precise and efficient. Kael sat apart, his gaze fixed on the dying embers of the campfire, a grim silhouette against the encroaching twilight.

The Blood Moon, they knew, was fast approaching. Its crimson glow, a harbinger of ancient magic and heightened power, loomed like a malevolent deity in the near future. It was a time of heightened power for werewolves, but also a time of heightened vulnerability. Keegan, a master of dark magic, would undoubtedly seize this opportunity to unleash his full might against them. This upcoming night would be the final battle. Their survival depended on the meticulous planning and execution of their strategy.

"We need to reinforce the perimeter," Damian said, his voice rough. The words felt heavy, each syllable laden with the weight of responsibility. He looked at Kael, his most trusted warrior, the man who had stood by him through thick and thin. The betrayal had cut deep, leaving scars that time alone couldn't heal. Yet, the remaining loyalty was unwavering, a stark contrast to the recently experienced turmoil.

Kael nodded, his eyes reflecting the dying firelight. "The outer defenses are weakened. The traitors... their actions have left gaps in our security." He paused, his voice filled with a quiet intensity. "We need to seal those gaps before Keegan exploits them."

The next few days were a whirlwind of activity. Lyra, with her uncanny ability to read the land, oversaw the reinforcement of the defensive positions. She directed the remaining pack members, her commands precise and efficient, her silver eyes missing nothing. Kael, along with several loyal warriors, meticulously patrolled the perimeter, setting traps and strengthening the wards that protected their sanctuary.

Damian, however, focused on the strategy itself. He spent hours poring over maps, studying Keegan's past movements, attempting to anticipate his next move. The impending battle wasn't just a physical confrontation; it was a war of wits, a contest of strategy and cunning. He knew that Keegan would exploit every weakness, every chink in their armor. The Blood Moon amplified magical abilities, including strategic thinking and intuitive abilities; Damian needed to harness that power.

He also dedicated time to rebuilding trust within the pack. The shadow of betrayal still lingered, a chilling presence that haunted their every interaction. He held council meetings, addressing the remaining members, emphasizing the importance of unity and the common goal they had to achieve. He focused on reaffirming their loyalty towards each other, and reminding them that they were a pack – a family bound by shared experiences and mutual respect.

The process was slow, arduous, but necessary. He spoke of forgiveness, acknowledging the pain and the violation of trust that the betrayers had caused, but stressing the need to move beyond the anger and towards a future where healing and unity could be restored. He spoke of the courage of Elara, who had risked everything to expose the conspiracy. He talked of the strength and resilience they had shown throughout their battles, and assured them that the same resilience would guide them in this upcoming fight.

He listened to their fears, their concerns, their doubts. He shared his own anxieties, his own uncertainties, in a move to build trust and ensure mutual transparency, creating an environment of openness and honesty that was essential for their collective survival. These were long conversations, deep discussions that went beyond strategic planning and touched upon the very soul of the Silvermoon Pack. It was a delicate dance of hope and despair, a test of his ability to lead, not only in battle but also in times of profound emotional upheaval.

As the Blood Moon drew nearer, the tension within the sanctuary became palpable. The atmosphere crackled with anticipation and anxiety, a silent hum of energy that vibrated through the very earth itself. The warriors sharpened their claws and teeth, their eyes gleaming with a primal intensity. The air itself seemed to hum with magical energy, a potent force that both excited and terrified them.

Damian felt the weight of the coming battle pressing down on him. The responsibility of leading his pack rested heavily on his shoulders, a burden he bore with a grim determination. He knew that the Blood Moon would amplify their strengths, but it would also magnify their weaknesses. It would be a night of heightened emotions, of amplified powers, and of ultimate decisions. This night was a defining moment in their history.

Their strategy was meticulously crafted, taking into account every possible scenario. They would defend their sanctuary, relying on traps, wards, and the element of surprise. They wouldn't engage in direct confrontation unless necessary. Their priority was to survive and regroup. Damian knew the Blood Moon wouldn't just heighten their powers; it would also strengthen Keegan's. They couldn't win a straight fight. They had to use their cunning, their intelligence, their knowledge of the terrain to their advantage.

The night of the Blood Moon arrived cloaked in an ominous silence, broken only by the rustling of leaves and the distant howl of a lone wolf. The crimson glow of the moon cast an eerie light upon the landscape, transforming the familiar surroundings into a mystical realm of shadows and whispers. The air crackled with magical energy, a tangible force that heightened the senses, sharpening instincts and amplifying emotions. The warriors stood poised, ready for battle, their senses heightened, their hearts pounding in unison with the rhythm of the approaching storm. The final battle was about to begin. The fate of the Silvermoon Pack hung precariously in the balance, as did the destiny of all those who relied on them. The shadows danced, beckoning the beginning of the night of blood.

Chapter 3:
The Blood Moon Rises

The crimson disc of the Blood Moon hung heavy in the sky, its malevolent glow casting long, dancing shadows across the Silvermoon sanctuary. The air thrummed with a potent energy, a palpable hum that vibrated through the very ground beneath their feet. Damian felt it first, a tingling sensation that spread from his fingertips to the roots of his hair, a wave of power that both exhilarated and terrified him. He stood on the precipice of his full transformation, a metamorphosis that would define not only his future but the fate of his entire pack.

He had always felt the pull of the moon, the primal rhythm of his werewolf blood echoing the celestial cycles. But this was different. This was a transformation unlike any he had ever experienced, a surge of raw, untamed power that threatened to overwhelm him. He could feel the ancient magic of the Blood Moon coursing through his veins, igniting a fire in his soul, a potent force that seemed to rewrite his very being.

The first changes were subtle. A low growl rumbled deep in his chest, a primal sound that resonated with the ancient energy of the moon. His muscles tensed, corded with power, his senses sharpening to an almost unbearable degree. He could smell the pine needles on the wind, the damp earth beneath his feet, the faint scent of fear emanating from the pack members huddled around the perimeter. He could hear the rustle of leaves, the distant howl of a coyote, the erratic beating of his own heart. He could taste the metallic tang of blood – a lingering echo of the recent battles, a testament to their shared trials.

Then, the transformation accelerated. His bones cracked and shifted, reshaping his frame into something larger, more powerful, more... primal. His skin tingled, then burned, as thick, coarse fur erupted across his body, a dark, silver-grey that shimmered in the moonlight. His fingers and toes elongated, transforming into sharp, wicked claws, capable of tearing flesh and bone. His jaw lengthened, his teeth transforming into long, pointed canines, the teeth of a predator. His eyes, once a warm hazel, blazed with an intense, fiery gold, reflecting the crimson light of the moon.

The change was agonizing, excruciating, yet at the same time, strangely exhilarating. It was as if his very essence was being ripped apart and reforged, reborn into a creature of immense power. He felt his height increase, his muscles swelling to an unnatural size, filled with the strength and stamina of a creature born of the wild. His senses intensified further, expanding exponentially. He could smell the fear of his enemies from miles away, and he could feel the pulse of the Blood Moon's energy beating in perfect synchronicity with his own heart.

As the transformation neared its completion, the physical changes were accompanied by a wave of emotional intensity. Damian felt a surge of primal rage, a ferocious instinct to hunt, to conquer, to destroy. It was a wild, untamed power, a potent force that could easily consume him if he wasn't careful. He struggled to maintain control, to keep the beast at bay. His mind, usually sharp and strategic, was clouded by a wave of instinctual urges.

He fought to retain his human intellect, to hold onto the memories of Lyra, Kael, Elara, and the rest of his pack. The memories of their shared struggles, the bond of brotherhood, the hope for a future free from Keegan's tyranny – these were the anchors that kept him grounded, preventing him from succumbing to the complete dominance of his werewolf instincts. He clutched these memories to his soul, using them as a shield against the overwhelming tide of his primal nature.

The pain subsided, replaced by a sense of immense power. He stood tall, a magnificent creature of both power and grace. His fur shimmered in the moonlight, his eyes blazed, his muscles rippled with barely contained energy. He was a warrior, a protector, a leader. He was Damian, but transformed. He was the embodiment of the Silvermoon Pack's strength, their resilience, their unwavering spirit.

But the transformation was not without its consequences. The heightened senses brought with them an amplified awareness of the fear and anxiety surrounding him. He felt the weight of his responsibilities, the burden of leadership, the fear of his pack members. He felt the immense power that coursed through his veins, a potent force that could easily be turned against him, and used against his people.

His heightened senses made him aware of the subtle shifts in the energy surrounding him. He could feel the presence of Keegan's dark magic pulsing in the distance, a malevolent force that threatened to consume them all. He could feel the unspoken fears of his pack, the silent anxieties that permeated their huddled forms. He could feel the weight of their hopes and dreams resting heavily on his shoulders.

This was not just a physical transformation; it was a spiritual one. He was no longer just a man; he was something more, something ancient, something powerful. But with this newfound power came a profound responsibility. He was now the protector of his pack, the guardian of their sanctuary, the leader who must guide them through the coming battle.

The weight of this responsibility was almost crushing, but Damian bore it with a grim determination. He would not falter. He would not fail. He would face Keegan, he would protect his pack, and he would survive the night of the Blood Moon. He would lead them to victory, or he would die trying. The transformation was complete. He was ready. The final battle awaited. And as the crimson glow of the Blood Moon illuminated his transformed form, Damian felt a chilling certainty: tonight, the fate of the Silvermoon Pack would be decided. The night of blood had truly begun. The shadows whispered promises of destruction and renewal, and Damian stood ready to meet his destiny. The scent of impending battle filled his heightened senses, the primal urges stirring within him, but he held firm, his heart beating in time with the rhythm of the blood moon, his eyes fixed on the horizon, awaiting the arrival of his enemy. The night was young, and the fight had just begun.

The air crackled with anticipation, the silence broken only by the frantic thumping of Damian's heart and the eerie whisper of the wind through the gnarled branches of the ancient oak trees. He stood poised, his enhanced senses painting a vivid picture of the approaching threat. Keegan's presence was a palpable wave of darkness, a chilling aura that chilled him to the bone despite the searing heat of the Blood Moon's crimson glow. He smelled the sharp tang of iron and sulfur, a scent that clung to Keegan like a shroud, a testament to the dark magic that fueled his power.

He saw him then, emerging from the shadows like a phantom, Keegan's form silhouetted against the crimson backdrop of the moon. His eyes, burning with a malevolent green light, locked onto Damian's, a silent challenge passing between them. Keegan was tall and imposing, his dark robes billowing around him like a storm cloud, his hands clenched into fists, crackling with dark energy. He carried himself with a chilling arrogance, a self-assuredness born from years of unchecked power and merciless conquest.

The ground trembled beneath their feet as they charged toward each other, a clash of titans heralding the beginning of their epic confrontation. Damian moved with a speed and agility that belied his size, his werewolf instincts honed to a razor's edge. Keegan, on the other hand, relied on raw, untamed power, his movements less refined but imbued with an overwhelming force.

Their first collision was a shockwave of raw energy, a deafening roar that shattered the night's silence. Damian's claws ripped into Keegan's robes, but the dark magic protecting him deflected the blow, sending sparks flying. Keegan retaliated with a blast of dark energy, a searing wave of black fire that scorched Damian's fur, the searing heat almost unbearable. Damian roared in defiance, his enhanced senses allowing him to anticipate Keegan's next move, dodging a second blast with ease.

The battle escalated into a whirlwind of blows, a brutal dance of destruction played out beneath the watchful gaze of the Blood

Moon. Damian fought with the ferocity of a cornered wolf, his speed and agility allowing him to evade Keegan's powerful attacks while landing swift, precise strikes of his own. His claws tore at Keegan's defenses, leaving deep gashes in his robes, drawing beads of blood. Keegan's strikes were less precise, but brutal in their force, each blow carrying enough power to shatter stone. The air around them crackled with energy, the clash of their powers creating an electric storm.

Damian's heightened senses were his greatest advantage. He could anticipate Keegan's movements before they were made, anticipating his every shift and feint. He smelled the fear masking the dark mage's arrogance, a subtle scent that gave him a slight edge. He could hear the subtle creaks and shifts in Keegan's defenses, the almost imperceptible sounds of his magic straining under the assault. He tasted the metallic tang of blood, both his own and Keegan's, mingling on the wind. Each sense was a weapon, helping him to strategize, to adapt, and to survive.

Keegan, however, was no slouch. His dark magic was a powerful weapon, capable of devastating blows and shielding him from Damian's attacks. He summoned shadows to ensnare Damian, whips of darkness that lashed out and tore at his flesh. He unleashed bolts of dark energy, blasts of concentrated power that seared Damian's skin. He summoned creatures of shadow, monstrous beings that tore at Damian with clawed hands and sharp teeth.

The battle raged across the sanctuary, leaving a trail of destruction in its wake. Trees were uprooted, rocks shattered, and the very earth trembled under the force of their conflict. Damian fought with relentless determination, his will fueled by the desire to protect his pack, to secure their future. He fought for Lyra, for Kael, for Elara, for the hope of a brighter tomorrow.

As the battle wore on, both Damian and Keegan began to tire, their energies waning. Damian felt the strain on his muscles, the exhaustion threatening to overwhelm him. But the primal energy of the Blood Moon coursed through his veins, replenishing his strength, pushing him onward. Keegan, however, seemed to draw strength from the very darkness surrounding them, his magic seeming to grow stronger as the night deepened.

Damian unleashed a desperate attack, a flurry of blows that caught Keegan off guard. His claws ripped through Keegan's defenses, leaving him bleeding and wounded. But Keegan retaliated with a final, desperate blast of dark magic, a surge of power so immense that it sent Damian reeling, throwing him back against a large oak tree, cracking its ancient branches.

Damian lay stunned, the wind knocked out of him. He felt a searing pain in his side, a deep gash that bled freely. He could barely breathe, his vision blurring. He looked up to see Keegan standing over him, a triumphant glint in his eyes, his hand raised to deliver the final blow. But just as Keegan was about to strike, a piercing howl cut through the night, the sound echoing across the sanctuary. A wave of energy washed over them, a surge of power that both men felt, the air itself seeming to tremble. The ground shook violently, and a deafening roar filled the air. It seemed as if the very sanctuary held its breath in anticipation, as if the earth itself was unwilling to witness the end of the confrontation. The fate of their conflict was still hanging in the balance, decided not solely by their strength and magical abilities, but by the forces at play beneath the crimson light of the Blood Moon. The tension was unbearable, the uncertainty palpable in the silence which followed the echoing howl.

The piercing howl reverberated through Damian's battered body, a shockwave of sound that resonated deep within his bones. He felt a surge of power, a revitalizing energy that pulsed through his veins, momentarily pushing back the crippling pain in his side. Keegan, momentarily stunned by the unexpected interruption, lowered his hand, his triumphant expression replaced by a look of wary suspicion.

The source of the howl was impossible to discern in the immediate darkness, but the ground continued to tremble, hinting at a force far greater than either he or Keegan possessed. Then, from the shadows at the edge of the sanctuary, figures began to emerge. Not the shadowy creatures Keegan commanded, but beings of light and energy, their forms shimmering and indistinct in the crimson glow of the Blood Moon.

First came Elara, her eyes blazing with an unearthly light, her hands raised, channeling a torrent of pure, white energy. The energy coalesced into a shimmering shield, protecting Damian from Keegan's vengeful gaze. Beside her stood Kael, his usually stoic face etched with grim determination. He wasn't wielding any weapon, but his very presence radiated a power that seemed to ripple outwards, reinforcing Elara's shield. Their combined power created an aura of resilience, a fortress of light that stood defiant against the encroaching darkness.

Behind them, even more unexpected allies materialized: a small band of villagers, their faces illuminated by a fierce determination that belied their normally quiet demeanor. They weren't warriors, not physically strong, but their courage was undeniable. They held aloft crudely fashioned torches, their flickering flames creating a stark contrast to the overwhelming darkness. But it wasn't just the light of the torches that seemed significant; a low hum resonated from them, a subtle vibration that amplified Elara and Kael's protective energies.

And then, a figure emerged from the deeper recesses of the sanctuary, a figure Damian hadn't seen in years, a figure he thought lost to time. Old Man Hemlock, the village healer, the man who had taught Damian much of what he knew about the balance of nature and the subtle energies that flowed through the world. Hemlock, frail and bent with age, now stood tall, his eyes shining with an unexpected intensity. He carried a simple wooden staff, but in his hands it glowed with an ancient, ethereal power, its luminescence pulsing in rhythm with the ground's tremor.

He raised his staff, and a wave of emerald green energy washed over Damian, healing the deep gash in his side. The searing pain receded, replaced by a soothing warmth that revitalized his body. The villagers' hum intensified, their collective energy merging with Hemlock's, bolstering Damian's renewed strength. It was a symphony of power, a testament to the strength of community, a force far greater than the sum of its parts.

Keegan watched, his arrogance faltering for the first time. He had anticipated a fight, a brutal duel against a lone werewolf. He hadn't anticipated this – a united front, a wave of unexpected allies, bolstering each other's strengths, creating an impenetrable shield of light against his dark magic. The balance had shifted, the odds dramatically altered. The villagers' presence, initially seeming insignificant, had amplified the energies of the more powerful allies, creating a synergistic effect that surprised even Damian.

The dark energy crackling around Keegan seemed to flicker and dim under the onslaught of this unexpected alliance. His confident demeanor wavered, his eyes darting between the various sources of resistance, his dark magic struggling to maintain its dominance. The overwhelming power of the combined energies left him visibly unsettled. The subtle energies Hemlock channeled flowed into the ground, subtly shifting the landscape, disrupting Keegan's ability to draw strength from the earth itself.

Elara, her eyes alight with fierce determination, unleashed another wave of energy, a searing blast of white light that struck Keegan squarely in the chest. He staggered back, his dark robes billowing around him, his face contorted in pain. Kael, seizing the opportunity, stepped forward, his very presence creating a sense of overwhelming pressure, a force that seemed to crush Keegan's will. The villagers, chanting in unison, intensified their hum, bolstering the energy radiating from Elara and Kael.

Keegan tried to retaliate, summoning shadowy tendrils to lash out at his attackers, but the combined defenses held firm. The shadows were repelled, dissipating against the shimmering shield of light. The ground beneath his feet trembled, the ancient power of the sanctuary itself seemingly turning against him, as if the earth itself was unwilling to support his dark magic any longer.

The battle had transformed. It was no longer a lone wolf against a dark mage, but a community standing united against a common threat. The villagers' simple torches, their unwavering courage, amplified the powers of Elara, Kael, and Hemlock, creating a synergy that surprised even Damian. Their collective will, woven together with the ancient energies of the sanctuary, was proving to be an insurmountable force.

The combined energies created a powerful vortex of light and sound, pushing back against Keegan's darkness. He struggled against it, his dark magic straining under the pressure. The very air crackled with the clash of opposing forces, a tempest of energy that threatened to tear the sanctuary apart. Keegan, for the first time, looked truly vulnerable, his power waning under the combined might of his unexpected foes.

He attempted another desperate surge of dark magic, a final attempt to reclaim dominance, but the collective energy of the villagers, combined with the sheer force of Elara and Kael's abilities and Hemlock's ancient knowledge, repelled his attack. The intensity of the light was blinding, the combined energy creating a blinding white light that seemed to momentarily overwhelm even the crimson glow of the Blood Moon.

The tide had turned. The unexpected alliance, forged in the crucible of battle, had proven to be far stronger than any single entity could have been. The battle was far from over, but the balance had shifted irrevocably. The unexpected allies, emerging from the seemingly insignificant corners of Damian's world, had rewritten the narrative, transforming a seemingly hopeless battle into a contest of hope and collective strength. Their combined strength, their unwavering courage, was the key that could unlock victory, turning the tide against the encroaching darkness. The unexpected allies, once unseen, unacknowledged, were now the unwavering pillars upon which Damian's hope rested, a testament to the power of community and the unexpected strength hidden within the seemingly ordinary. The night continued, filled with the clash of magic and the roar of determined allies, a night where the crimson glow of the Blood Moon witnessed not only a desperate struggle but also the unexpected blossoming of a powerful alliance, a testament to the indomitable spirit of unity and the strength found in the most unlikely of bonds. Underneath the crimson light of the Blood Moon, the battle raged on, but it was no longer a lone wolf fighting a dark mage; it was a community united against the darkness, their strength magnified by the unexpected alliance forged under the ominous glow.

The crimson glow of the Blood Moon cast long, dancing shadows as the battle intensified. Keegan, weakened but not broken, unleashed a torrent of dark energy, a desperate attempt to reclaim control. The shadowy tendrils lashed out, seeking to pierce the shimmering shield protecting Damian and his allies. Elara, her face strained with exertion, channeled more power into the barrier, her breath coming in ragged gasps. Kael, a wall of unwavering resolve, stood firm, his presence a palpable weight pressing down on Keegan. The villagers, their faces etched with fear and determination, continued their rhythmic hum, their collective energy a vital component of the protective shield.

Then, a horrifying shriek pierced the air. One of the villagers, a young woman named Lyra, stumbled, her hand clutching her chest. The protective shield flickered, momentarily weakening, and a dark tendril snaked past Elara's defenses, striking Lyra with brutal force. She collapsed, her body convulsing, the light fading from her eyes. A collective gasp rippled through the remaining villagers, their hum faltering, their strength momentarily broken.

The loss of Lyra was a devastating blow. It was a stark reminder of the cost of their defiance, a tangible sacrifice in their fight against the encroaching darkness. Damian felt a wave of grief and guilt wash over him. He had led them into this battle, and now one of his allies had paid the ultimate price. The weight of responsibility pressed down on him, a crushing burden that threatened to overwhelm him. He looked at the faces of the remaining villagers, their expressions a mixture of sorrow and unwavering determination. He saw the flicker of fear in their eyes, but beneath it lay an unyielding resolve, a testament to their courage in the face of unimaginable loss.

Hemlock, his face etched with sorrow, stepped forward, his wooden staff glowing with a soft emerald light. He placed his hand on Lyra's still form, his ancient magic flowing into her body in a desperate attempt to revive her. But the darkness had taken too firm a hold; the life had already fled her eyes. His shoulders slumped, his age showing in the profound weariness of his posture. Even his considerable magic couldn't reverse the damage. The silence that followed Lyra's death was deafening, broken only by the crackling of conflicting energies and Keegan's sinister laughter.

The loss of Lyra fueled a new fire in the hearts of the remaining villagers. Their fear was replaced by righteous anger, a burning resentment against the darkness that had stolen their friend's life. Their hum intensified, a testament to their grief and fury. The collective energy surged, bolstering Elara and Kael's defenses. The shield, though weakened, held firm.

Keegan, sensing the shift in momentum, redoubled his efforts. He summoned a storm of dark energy, a vortex of shadows that threatened to overwhelm them. Elara, summoning every ounce of her strength, fought back, her white energy clashing against the encroaching darkness. The sanctuary trembled, the ground shaking under the force of the conflicting magic.

Damian, spurred by a mixture of grief and rage, joined the fray. He unleashed his own werewolf abilities, his claws extending, his teeth bared in a snarl. He fought with a ferocity he hadn't known he possessed, his pain and sorrow fueling his actions. His howls echoed Keegan's, yet they were different – his were filled with raw emotion, with the burning pain of loss and the unyielding determination to avenge Lyra's death.

The battle raged on, a brutal dance of light and shadow, of life and death. Each blow landed with the weight of their shared sorrow and the burning desire for vengeance. As they fought, Damian could feel the strain in his allies, the exhaustion slowly creeping into their movements. Elara's energy began to wane, her light dimming slightly under the constant onslaught. Kael's unwavering resolve was starting to show cracks; the pressure was starting to take its toll. Even Hemlock, despite his ancient power, was slowing, his emerald glow flickering and fading, his breath labored.

Despite the waning strength of his allies, they pressed on, their courage fueled by grief and the shared responsibility to protect their world. They understood the dire consequences of defeat, the destruction of everything they held dear. Each strike they landed was not only an attempt to overcome Keegan, but to honor the sacrifice Lyra made. It was a battle fought not just for survival, but for the memory of a fallen friend. Their combined strength, though thinning, was still stronger than Keegan's waning power, their collective will refusing to be broken.

The tide, however, began to turn. Keegan, weakened but still cunning, began to exploit the cracks in their defenses. He targeted Kael, launching a concentrated burst of dark energy that caught him off guard. Kael stumbled, his aura wavering, his protective presence faltering. The shield protecting Damian faltered, and a tendril of dark energy lashed out, grazing Damian's arm. The pain was sharp, a searing reminder of his own vulnerability.

Hemlock, seeing Kael fall, desperately tried to bolster his ally, using his remaining magic to revitalize Kael's strength. He, too, fell. A searing blast of dark energy struck him directly, sending him crashing to the ground. His body lay still, the emerald glow of his staff extinguished. The silence that followed was more profound this time, heavier. Two sacrifices had been made, two losses adding to the cost of their fight. The despair was almost palpable, threatening to overwhelm the remaining allies.

The villagers' humming slowed, the collective energy weakening. Elara, her face pale and her breath coming in gasps, continued to fight, but even her strength was waning fast. The shield flickered, wavering under the relentless assault of Keegan's dark magic.

Damian looked at Elara, at the exhausted villagers, and felt a surge of despair. Lyra and Hemlock were gone. Kael was injured and the remaining allies were nearing exhaustion. He knew they were losing. But even as despair threatened to engulf him, he saw a flicker of defiance in Elara's eyes. She looked at him, her gaze filled with unwavering determination.

And in that moment, Damian understood. The battle wasn't solely about winning or losing, about survival or destruction. It was about standing tall, about fighting with everything you had, even when the odds were insurmountable. It was about honoring the sacrifices made by Lyra and Hemlock, about carrying their memory into the heart of the coming fight. It was about the unwavering spirit of courage, the defiance that bloomed even in the face of certain defeat. It was a testament to the indomitable spirit of unity and resilience in the face of insurmountable odds. The night raged on, the final battle unfolding under the watchful gaze of the crimson Blood Moon. The weight of their losses was heavy, but the fire of their determination burned even brighter.

The crimson moon hung heavy in the sky, a malevolent eye witnessing the aftermath of the brutal battle. Elara, her face streaked with grime and sweat, slumped against a shattered stone, her breath ragged. Damian, his werewolf form still flickering with residual power, cradled Kael's head in his lap, the older werewolf's breathing shallow and erratic. The sanctuary lay in ruins, a testament to the ferocity of the conflict. The air, thick with the scent of blood and burnt magic, hummed with a lingering tension.

Lyra and Hemlock, their lives sacrificed on the altar of defiance, lay still amongst the rubble, a stark reminder of the terrible cost of their resistance.

The silence that followed was deafening, broken only by the occasional groan from the injured. The villagers, their faces etched with grief and exhaustion, huddled together, their collective energy depleted, a faint, melancholic hum the only sign of their remaining strength. Keegan was gone, vanquished, but the victory felt hollow, tainted by the heavy price they had paid.

Damian looked at the devastation around him, at the faces of his allies, their eyes reflecting the weight of their losses. He felt the familiar ache of his own wounds, the sharp sting of the dark energy that had grazed his arm. But physical pain paled in comparison to the emotional toll. He had lost two dear friends, two pillars of strength, and the weight of their deaths pressed down on him with crushing force.

The immediate aftermath was a blur of tending to the wounded, a frantic effort to salvage what little remained. The villagers, despite their exhaustion, worked tirelessly, tending to the injured, supporting each other, their actions a silent testament to their unwavering resilience. Elara, though weakened, used her remaining magic to heal the less severe injuries, her touch gentle yet powerful. Kael, slowly regaining consciousness, muttered words of thanks, his voice weak but his eyes filled with gratitude.

As dawn broke, painting the ravaged sanctuary in hues of somber grey and pale orange, the reality of their victory, or rather, their survival, sunk in. The power dynamics within the werewolf world had irrevocably shifted. Keegan's fall had left a vacuum, a power void that would inevitably be filled. The various werewolf clans, previously bound by a fragile truce under Keegan's iron fist, now looked to forge new alliances, to secure their positions in this newly chaotic landscape.

Damian, despite his grief, found himself thrust into a position of unexpected leadership. His courage, his unwavering resolve in the face of overwhelming odds, had earned him the respect, even the reverence, of the remaining villagers and the surviving members of his own pack. He was no longer just a young werewolf, battling to survive. He was a symbol of hope, a leader forged in the crucible of loss and sacrifice.

The news of Keegan's defeat spread like wildfire through the werewolf world. Some clans rejoiced, seeing the end of Keegan's tyrannical rule as an opportunity for liberation. Others mourned the loss of their powerful leader, fearing the ensuing chaos. The ensuing power struggle was brutal, a complex dance of shifting alliances and bitter betrayals. Clans that had once been enemies found common ground, forging uneasy alliances against those who sought to exploit the vacuum of power.

Damian, now recognized as a powerful leader, received numerous offers of allegiance. He carefully considered each proposition, weighing the strength and loyalty of each clan, assessing their potential contribution to the new order. He knew that rebuilding would take time, that the wounds inflicted during the battle were deep and would require patience and skillful leadership.

One of the most significant shifts in power concerned the Elder Council, a group of ancient and powerful werewolves traditionally responsible for maintaining peace and order within the werewolf world. The council, weakened by Keegan's reign of terror, had been largely sidelined, its influence diminished. Damian, with the support of the remaining villagers and his loyal pack members, worked to restore the council's power, ensuring it was reformed with individuals who shared his vision of a more just and equitable society. This decision was met with both celebration and resistance, some clans wary of entrusting their fate to a relatively young werewolf, while others saw it as a necessary step in restoring balance.

The transformation wasn't merely political; it was a spiritual one. The combined sacrifice of Lyra and Hemlock, their unwavering courage in the face of death, had created a ripple effect, awakening a latent power within the remaining villagers. They were no longer simply passive participants in the larger conflict, but active agents of change, their collective energy, sharpened by loss and infused with newfound resolve, now a force to be reckoned with. Their songs, once used to strengthen the protective barrier, were now anthems of defiance and resilience, echoing throughout the forests, inspiring others to rise against tyranny.

The rebuilding process was far from easy. The land was scarred, the people were grieving, and the future remained uncertain. Damian faced numerous challenges: managing the rebuilding efforts, navigating the complex political landscape of the werewolf clans, and dealing with the lingering effects of Keegan's dark magic. He also had to grapple with his own personal grief, the weight of responsibility pressing down on him with unrelenting force.

Yet, despite the hardships, a new sense of unity emerged. The shared experience of loss forged a bond stronger than any previous alliance. The villagers and the various werewolf packs, once disparate entities, were now inextricably linked, their fates intertwined. They had faced their darkest hour, and in doing so, had discovered a strength within themselves they never knew existed.

The Blood Moon, once a symbol of impending doom, now shone with a different light, a faint glow of hope amidst the ruins. The night of the battle marked not just an end, but a new beginning, a turning point in the werewolf world. The power dynamics had shifted, the leadership reformed, and the future, though uncertain, held the promise of a new dawn, a dawn tempered by loss but fueled by the indomitable spirit of those who had survived. The landscape of power had been reshaped, the foundation laid for a future where the strength of unity, not the tyranny of brute force, would define the werewolf world. The journey ahead was long and arduous, but under Damian's leadership, and with the support of his allies, there was a glimmer of hope, a promise of a brighter tomorrow, etched against the backdrop of the fading crimson glow of the Blood Moon. The echoes of their battle, the sacrifices made, would forever resonate, shaping the new world order, a testament to the strength found in unity, and the resilience of the human spirit.

Chapter 4:
The Aftermath

The first rays of dawn painted the ravaged sanctuary in hues of bruised purple and ashen grey, a stark contrast to the crimson horror of the night before. The air, still thick with the scent of blood and burnt magic, held a chilling stillness, broken only by the soft whimpers of the injured and the occasional sigh of the exhausted. Elara, her face pale but resolute, moved amongst the wounded, her hands glowing with a gentle, ethereal light as she mended broken bones and soothed ravaged flesh. Her magic, though depleted, was a beacon of hope in the desolate landscape. She worked tirelessly, her movements precise and efficient, her exhaustion masked by a steely determination. Each touch was a silent prayer, a whisper of healing against the deafening silence of loss.

Damian, still in his partially shifted werewolf form, watched her with a mixture of gratitude and sorrow. The residual magic throbbed in his veins, a dull ache that mirrored the throbbing pain in his heart. Kael, his mentor and friend, lay still in his arms, his breathing shallow and uneven. The older werewolf's strength, usually a comforting presence, was now fragile, a whisper against the harsh reality of their victory. Damian gently stroked Kael's fur, whispering words of comfort and reassurance, though he felt a hollowness inside that no words could fill. Lyra and Hemlock's absence was a gaping wound in the fabric of his being, a constant, agonizing reminder of their sacrifice.

The villagers, their faces etched with exhaustion and grief, moved around them like phantoms, their actions a testament to their enduring spirit. They shared food, water, and murmured words of support. Despite the devastation, they were a community bound by loss, their collective grief forming an unexpected bond of resilience. They were the living embodiment of the words 'enduring spirit', their quiet determination a testament to their strength.

As the sun climbed higher, casting long, skeletal shadows across the ravaged land, Damian finally allowed himself a moment of quiet reflection. He sat beside Kael, the weight of the battle settling heavily upon him. The physical wounds were healing, thanks to Elara's skillful magic, but the emotional scars were far deeper, far more intractable. He felt the familiar sting of guilt, the weight of the lives lost. Had he done everything he could? Could he have prevented Lyra and Hemlock's deaths? The questions gnawed at him, leaving him with a sense of unbearable responsibility.

He closed his eyes, the images of the battle flashing before him like a broken film reel: Lyra's fierce defiance, Hemlock's unwavering loyalty, Keegan's cruel laughter as he unleashed his dark magic. The memories were vivid, brutal reminders of the price they had paid for their hard-won victory. He saw the faces of the fallen, their eyes reflecting a courage that would forever inspire him.

Opening his eyes, he looked out at the devastation around him. The sanctuary, once a place of peace and sanctuary, was now a graveyard of broken stones and shattered dreams. But even amid the ruins, there was a flicker of hope, a fragile ember of resilience. The villagers, despite their losses, were already beginning to clear the rubble, their actions a testament to their indomitable spirit.

It was then that Damian truly understood the weight of his new role. He was no longer just a young werewolf fighting for survival. He was a leader, responsible for the lives of those who had survived the battle, responsible for guiding them through the darkness and into a brighter future. The responsibility felt crushing, a weight that threatened to suffocate him. But within that burden, he also found a new source of strength, a renewed resolve to honor the sacrifices of those he had lost.

The days that followed were a blur of activity. The wounded were cared for, the dead were mourned, and the work of rebuilding began. Damian, drawing strength from his allies and the unwavering spirit of the villagers, guided the efforts, his decisions tempered by his grief and fueled by his resolve. He was no longer just a warrior; he was a leader, a shepherd leading his flock into an uncertain future.

He spent hours in quiet contemplation, allowing himself to grieve, to acknowledge the pain and loss. He talked to Kael, who slowly recovered, sharing his burdens and seeking guidance from the wise old werewolf. He found solace in the simple acts of helping others, in the shared grief and mutual support that bound the community together.

The reconstruction was painstaking and slow. Each stone placed was a testament to their resilience, each step forward a small victory against despair. The rebuilding went beyond the physical structures; it was also about mending the fractured spirits of the community, about weaving back the threads of unity and trust that had been torn apart by Keegan's reign of terror.

He worked alongside Elara, their shared grief forging a deeper bond between them. Her magic was a constant source of comfort, her presence a soothing balm to his wounded soul. They spoke little, but their shared understanding transcended words. They were healers, both physically and emotionally, stitching together a community that had been shattered, and gradually finding healing themselves in the act of tending to others.

The political landscape, however, remained treacherous. The news of Keegan's defeat had spread like wildfire, causing ripples of uncertainty and fear through the werewolf world. Alliances shifted, rivalries flared, and new power struggles emerged. Damian faced numerous challenges: negotiating with rival clans, dealing with internal conflicts, and the ever-present threat of those seeking to exploit the power vacuum left by Keegan. He worked tirelessly, his days filled with meetings, negotiations, and the constant weighing of difficult decisions.

But through it all, he held onto the vision of a brighter future, a world where unity, not tyranny, would prevail. He remembered Lyra and Hemlock's sacrifice, their unwavering belief in a better world. Their memory fueled his resolve, providing him with the strength to overcome the obstacles that lay ahead.

The healing process was long and arduous, but under Damian's steady leadership, the community began to heal. The scars would remain, but they were gradually being transformed from wounds of despair into emblems of resilience. The memory of the fallen would be forever etched in their hearts, a constant reminder of the price of freedom and the strength found in unity. The crimson moon, once a symbol of doom, now served as a reminder of their hard-fought victory, the promise of a new dawn. A dawn of unity, of hope, and of a future built on the foundations of shared sacrifice and unwavering resilience. The echoes of the battle would continue to resonate, but now they would be a song of defiance, resilience, and renewal— a testament to the strength found in unity, and the indomitable spirit of those who had survived.

The whispers of dissent were subtle at first, a rustle in the undergrowth of the newly formed peace. Old rivalries, dormant under Keegan's iron fist, reemerged like poisonous weeds, choking the fragile shoots of unity. Damian, still bearing the fresh wounds of battle, both physical and emotional, found himself navigating a treacherous political landscape as complex as the tangled forests surrounding his newly inherited territory. His leadership, forged in the crucible of war, was now tested in the quieter, but equally dangerous, arena of diplomacy and power consolidation.

His first act was to address the immediate needs of the pack. Food was scarce, shelter inadequate, and the threat of disease loomed large. He initiated a system of rationing, ensuring fair distribution of resources, a task that required him to make unpopular decisions, incurring the wrath of some of the more powerful, and less scrupulous, members of the pack. He faced down their challenges, his voice calm but firm, his eyes reflecting the unwavering resolve he had honed on the battlefield. His authority, though new, was backed by the respect earned through his courage and leadership during the fight against Keegan.

The rebuilding of the sanctuary was his next priority. More than just stones and timber, it symbolized the rebuilding of their community, their collective spirit. He organized the work, delegating tasks based on each werewolf's strengths and abilities, fostering a sense of cooperation and shared purpose. The task was immense, the scars of the battle deeply etched in the very landscape. But under Damian's guidance, the pack worked with a newfound purpose, their efforts fuelled by a collective desire to reclaim their home, a testament to their resilience.

Then came the alliances. The neighboring werewolf clans, once hesitant allies, watched Damian's ascent with a mixture of apprehension and curiosity. Some saw him as a young, inexperienced leader, vulnerable and easily manipulated. Others sensed the strength, the quiet determination that lay beneath his calm exterior. Damian understood this dynamic, and he played it carefully. He offered no empty promises, no grandiose displays of power. Instead, he presented a vision of mutual benefit, a future where all clans could thrive, free from Keegan's tyranny.

His first negotiation was with the ShadowClan, a notoriously ruthless clan known for their cunning and strategic prowess. Their leader, a grizzled veteran named Morwen, was a formidable opponent, her eyes sharp as obsidian, her demeanor radiating an aura of cold authority. Damian met her in the neutral ground of a moonlit clearing, the ancient oaks casting long shadows around them. The air crackled with unspoken tensions, the scent of rivalry thick in the air.

The negotiation lasted for hours, a delicate dance of words and subtle threats. Damian offered a peace treaty, a mutual non-aggression pact, in exchange for the ShadowClan's support in securing the surrounding territories and ensuring stability. Morwen, initially reluctant, was slowly swayed by Damian's calm demeanor and his unwavering resolve. She saw a strength in him, a resilience that mirrored her own, and a vision for the future that could benefit all clans.

The treaty was signed under the watchful gaze of the silent trees, a fragile agreement sealed with a shared understanding of mutual need and respect. It was a significant victory for Damian, a testament to his diplomatic skills and his ability to navigate the treacherous currents of werewolf politics. It demonstrated his capacity to move beyond mere strength and establish a foundation built on respect, strategy, and a future where all could prosper, rather than be threatened.

However, other clans remained skeptical. The Iron Fang clan, led by the ambitious and power-hungry Kael's rival, Ragnar, openly challenged Damian's authority. Ragnar, a powerful werewolf with a reputation for cruelty, saw Damian's rise as a threat to his own ambitions, viewing the young leader as weak and easily manipulated, an opportunity for him to seize power for himself. He fomented dissent within Damian's own pack, spreading rumors and stirring up unrest.

Damian, aware of Ragnar's machinations, dealt with the threat decisively. He didn't resort to violence. Instead, he used his intelligence, carefully exposing Ragnar's lies and manipulative tactics. He held a council meeting, allowing the disgruntled members to voice their concerns. He listened patiently, his demeanor patient yet authoritative. He addressed each concern, offering logical explanations and solutions. Slowly but surely, he gained back the loyalty of those who had been swayed by Ragnar's lies. This was more than just a victory in a political game. It was a testament to his skills as a leader, his capacity to resolve conflicts peacefully and to cultivate the unity and support of his clan.

The clash with Ragnar ultimately resolved in a strategic standoff, a display of power without bloodshed. Damian proved his superior political acumen, exposing Ragnar's treachery and undermining his influence. The ensuing public disgrace served as a stark warning to any who dared to challenge his authority. He was not merely a warrior; he was a strategist, a politician, a leader capable of both commanding respect on the battlefield and navigating the intricate complexities of werewolf society.

The consolidation of Damian's power was not just a matter of military might or political maneuvering. It was a process of rebuilding trust, of fostering unity, and of inspiring hope in a community scarred by violence and loss. The reconstruction of the sanctuary was not just about rebuilding stones and timber. It was a symbol of his commitment, and the pack's, to forge a stronger, more resilient society. The alliances he forged were not merely strategic partnerships, they were the building blocks of a new era of cooperation and mutual prosperity amongst the werewolf clans.

The aftermath of Keegan's defeat was a time of immense challenges, but also a time of remarkable growth for Damian. He emerged from the ashes of war, not just as a leader of his pack, but as a symbol of hope for the entire werewolf community. The weight of his responsibility was immense, but so too was the strength he derived from his allies, from the unwavering spirit of his people, and from the memory of those who had sacrificed everything for the cause of freedom. He was a leader forged in fire, tempered by loss, and driven by an unyielding commitment to build a better future for his pack and for all werewolves. The reign of terror was over, and the dawn of a new era, one of unity and prosperity, was finally breaking.

The fragile peace, hard-won in the bloody battle against Keegan, felt less like a victory and more like a precarious balancing act. The wounds of war, both physical and emotional, ran deep within the pack. While the external threats had diminished, a new, insidious enemy had emerged: mistrust. The whispers of discontent, once faint murmurs, had grown into a chorus of doubt and suspicion. Many among the pack, hardened by years of Keegan's oppressive rule, found it difficult to relinquish their ingrained survival instincts, their ingrained suspicion of authority.

Liam, a grizzled veteran whose loyalty to Damian was unquestionable, approached him one evening, his face etched with worry. "The whispers are growing louder, Damian," Liam said, his voice low. "Many still question your leadership. They remember the old ways, the iron fist of Keegan. They don't trust this... this new era of peace."

Damian understood Liam's concern. He knew the shadow of Keegan's tyranny still loomed large over the pack, poisoning their minds with doubt. Keegan had ruled through fear, crushing dissent with brutal efficiency. To transition from that brutal reign to a more collaborative leadership style was a monumental task, demanding patience, understanding, and a willingness to address the deeply ingrained psychological scars of the past. The rebuilding of the sanctuary, the forging of alliances, these were tangible symbols of progress, yet they paled in comparison to the more subtle, more internal battles raging within the pack.

Elara, a fierce warrior known for her unmatched strength and loyalty, was one such source of internal conflict. While outwardly she pledged allegiance to Damian, her eyes held a flicker of skepticism, her silence a heavy weight in the halls of the newly rebuilt sanctuary. Her loyalty, tested by years of servitude to Keegan, was a fragile thing, easily swayed by doubt and uncertainty. She carried the weight of past trauma, the scars of Keegan's cruelty visible and invisible, and this had fostered a deep-seated mistrust, a reluctance to fully embrace Damian's more benevolent style of leadership.

Damian understood her skepticism. He knew that Elara's loyalty had to be earned, not demanded, and that earning it required a deeper understanding of her past experiences and her present fears. He sought her out, not in a grand display of authority, but in the quiet solitude of the forest. He engaged in a prolonged discussion, allowing Elara to air her grievances, her frustrations, and her fears without interruption.

"I understand your hesitation, Elara," he said, his voice gentle, understanding. "Keegan's rule was brutal, and the scars of his tyranny run deep. But we are building something new here, something different. A community based on trust, respect, and mutual support. It won't be easy, and it won't happen overnight, but it is our chance to create a better future, a future free from fear."

He spent hours listening to her, patiently unraveling the knots of her fear and resentment. He shared his own experiences, his own struggles, painting a picture of vulnerability that challenged the ingrained image of the strong, unyielding leader. This vulnerability became a key to forging a stronger connection, a deeper trust. It demonstrated that he was not above the vulnerabilities of his people, and that he, too, was burdened by the ghosts of the past.

Another challenge came from within the younger generation, who had known nothing but Keegan's oppressive rule. They had grown up fearing authority, viewing any form of leadership with inherent suspicion. Their youthful exuberance was tempered with a deep-seated cynicism, a mistrust bred by years of subjugation.

To overcome this, Damian understood that he needed to foster a sense of shared purpose, to provide them with a tangible sense of belonging and involvement. He established mentorship programs, pairing the younger members with experienced veterans, fostering bonds of respect and understanding. He delegated tasks to them, giving them a sense of responsibility and ownership within the pack. He actively listened to their ideas, showing that their voices held value, that they were essential contributors to the pack's success. He helped them channel their pent-up energy into productive activities, transforming their rebellious spirit into a drive for change and improvement.

This strategy worked gradually. Slowly, tentatively, the younger generation began to understand the importance of unity, of cooperation. They saw the tangible results of their collective effort, the slow but steady progress in rebuilding their sanctuary, their community, their lives.

The internal conflicts weren't always resolved through gentle conversation and shared purpose. There were moments of friction, of heated debate, of simmering resentment that threatened to boil over. Damian had to demonstrate his strength, his resolve, but always without resorting to violence. He learned to discern genuine dissent from manipulative tactics, to separate those who were genuinely conflicted from those who sought to undermine his authority for their own selfish gain.

The path to unity was long and arduous, fraught with setbacks and challenges. But with each obstacle overcome, with each conflict resolved, Damian's leadership grew stronger, more resilient, more deeply rooted in the trust and respect of his pack. He emerged not just as a powerful leader, but as a unifying force, a symbol of hope, of resilience, and of the possibility of a better future, a future free from the tyranny of the past. The reign of terror was indeed over, but the work of rebuilding, of healing the wounds of the past, was far from finished. The road ahead would be challenging, but with the unwavering support of his pack, Damian was ready to face whatever lay in store. The whispers of dissent were still there, but they were gradually fading, replaced by a growing chorus of hope and shared purpose. The new era was dawning, slowly but surely, born from the ashes of the past, forged in the crucible of conflict, and strengthened by the unwavering spirit of a pack united under the banner of a leader they had come to trust.

The scent of woodsmoke and fresh-turned earth hung heavy in the air, a stark contrast to the stench of blood and decay that had permeated the sanctuary just days before. The rebuilding was a tangible symbol of hope, a physical manifestation of Damian's promise of a new era. But the physical structures were only a small part of the larger, more complex process of healing. The wounds inflicted by Keegan's tyranny ran far deeper than cracked stone walls and splintered timber. They were etched into the very souls of the pack.

Damian, his own body bearing the scars of battle, understood this all too well. He didn't merely delegate the rebuilding efforts; he participated in them, his calloused hands working alongside his people, sharing the sweat and the strain, forging a bond of shared purpose. He meticulously oversaw the reconstruction of the training grounds, ensuring they were safer, better equipped, and more conducive to fostering camaraderie among the pack. He personally supervised the creation of a new infirmary, ensuring it was stocked with the necessary herbs and supplies, a stark improvement from the crude, under-resourced medical facilities under Keegan's rule. He even oversaw the construction of a community garden, a symbol of growth and renewal, a place where the pack could work together to cultivate not just food, but hope for the future.

Beyond the physical reconstruction, Damian focused on the emotional and psychological well-being of his pack. He established support groups, led by experienced healers and trusted veterans, where members could share their traumas, their fears, and their grief in a safe and supportive environment. These sessions weren't just about venting; they were about creating a sense of shared experience, a recognition that they were not alone in their suffering. He encouraged open dialogue, a stark contrast to the suffocating silence that had characterized Keegan's reign.

One of the most challenging aspects of the rebuilding process was addressing the deep-seated mistrust among the pack members. The scars of Keegan's tyranny were not easily erased, and the fear of betrayal lingered in their eyes. Damian knew that trust couldn't be demanded; it had to be earned. He began by dismantling the oppressive hierarchical structure that Keegan had imposed. He replaced it with a more collaborative and inclusive system, empowering individuals to contribute their unique skills and perspectives to the pack's collective effort. He held regular council meetings, ensuring everyone had a voice, no matter their rank or status. He listened patiently to their grievances, acknowledging their pain, validating their experiences, and promising to address their concerns.

Elara, despite her outward show of loyalty, remained a source of concern. Her taciturn nature and guarded demeanor spoke volumes about her lingering distrust. Damian approached her not with demands, but with understanding. He spent countless hours with her, engaging in quiet conversation, sharing stories of his own struggles and vulnerabilities. He revealed the scars on his own body, both physical and emotional, a testament to his own resilience and his understanding of their shared pain. He showed her that leadership wasn't about wielding power, but about serving the needs of the pack. Gradually, a tentative trust began to bloom between them, nurtured by shared experiences and mutual respect.

The younger generation presented a different set of challenges. Having known only Keegan's oppressive rule, they viewed authority with inherent suspicion. Their youthful exuberance was tempered by a deep-seated cynicism, a mistrust born out of years of oppression. Damian understood their skepticism, but he didn't dismiss it. He sought to engage them, to involve them in the rebuilding process, to give them a sense of ownership and purpose. He established a mentorship program, pairing the younger members with seasoned veterans, forging bonds of understanding and respect. He delegated responsibilities to them, allowing them to contribute their energy and ideas to the pack's collective efforts. He encouraged their creativity, their enthusiasm, channeling their youthful energy into productive activities.

He saw to the creation of a dedicated training area for the young pack members, focusing on cooperative exercises rather than the brutal, individualistic combat training favoured by Keegan. Teamwork was the new focus; unity was the new strength. He fostered a sense of belonging, providing them with a platform to express their concerns and contribute to the pack's future. He actively listened to their ideas, showing them that their voices mattered, that they were integral to the pack's success. He understood that they needed to be empowered, not controlled. And slowly, tentatively, their cynicism began to melt away, replaced by a growing sense of purpose and belonging.

The path to healing was not without its setbacks. There were moments of friction, of heated disagreements, of lingering resentments that threatened to boil over. Damian's leadership wasn't solely based on compassion; he demonstrated strength and resolve when necessary. He learned to distinguish between genuine dissent and manipulative tactics, separating those who were genuinely conflicted from those who sought to exploit the unrest for personal gain. He used diplomacy, but he also knew when a firm hand was required, always avoiding violence but asserting his authority when necessary.

He instituted a system of justice that was fair and transparent, ensuring accountability while emphasizing restorative practices over punitive ones. He worked to rebuild bridges between fractured families and clans, mending the deep divisions that Keegan's tyranny had created. He initiated cultural exchanges with neighboring communities, fostering alliances and promoting mutual understanding.

The process of healing was a marathon, not a sprint. There were days when progress felt imperceptible, when the whispers of doubt and suspicion threatened to overwhelm the burgeoning hope. But Damian persisted, driven by his unwavering commitment to his pack, his relentless pursuit of a better future.

Slowly, but surely, the wounds of the past began to heal. The whispers of discontent faded, replaced by a growing chorus of shared purpose and collective resilience. The sanctuary, once a symbol of oppression, transformed into a beacon of hope, a testament to the power of unity, compassion, and unwavering determination. The rebuilding was complete, not just of buildings and infrastructure, but of hearts and minds, of a community forged in the crucible of conflict, emerging stronger, more resilient, and united under the banner of a leader who had earned their trust and unwavering loyalty. The reign of terror was over, but the legacy of hope had just begun.

The first snowfall of the season dusted the rebuilt sanctuary in a pristine layer of white, a stark contrast to the scarred earth that had been its canvas just months before. The air, once thick with the stench of decay and fear, now carried the crisp scent of pine and the faint sweetness of woodsmoke from newly constructed hearths. The transformation was not just physical; it was a palpable shift in the collective spirit of the pack. A quiet confidence, a newfound resilience, emanated from the wolves, a subtle yet powerful testament to Damian's leadership.

The rebuilt training grounds hummed with activity. No longer a place of brutal competition and fear, it was a vibrant hub of cooperative training exercises. Young wolves, their faces alight with enthusiasm, practiced coordinated attacks, their movements fluid and synchronized, a stark contrast to the haphazard, individualistic combat that had characterized Keegan's regime. The air thrummed with the energy of shared purpose, the sound of laughter mingling with the rhythmic thud of paws on the packed earth. Damian, watching from a distance, felt a surge of pride. He hadn't just rebuilt a training ground; he'd rebuilt a sense of community.

The new infirmary, a spacious and well-lit structure, was a symbol of the pack's commitment to healing, both physical and emotional. Experienced healers, once relegated to the shadows under Keegan's rule, now held positions of respect and authority. They worked tirelessly, tending to both physical injuries and the lingering psychological wounds of the past. The herbal gardens, meticulously tended by the pack, provided a wealth of natural remedies, a testament to the integration of traditional knowledge with modern techniques. The air within the infirmary was infused with the scent of healing herbs, a comforting aroma that spoke of renewal and hope.

Evenings were now filled with a different sort of activity. The community hall, once a place of fear and intimidation, now resonated with music and laughter. Storytellers, their voices rich with the traditions of the pack, captivated their audience with tales of bravery, resilience, and the enduring spirit of the wolf. The younger generation, once cynical and distrustful, now actively participated, their faces illuminated by the flickering firelight and the warmth of shared experience. Damian, observing from a shadowed corner, noted the subtle changes. Their eyes, once clouded with suspicion, now shone with a nascent hope, a belief in the future they were building together.

Elara's transformation was among the most remarkable. The guarded demeanor, the quiet skepticism, had gradually faded, replaced by a quiet strength and a burgeoning sense of loyalty. She still maintained her independence, but her interactions with Damian were marked by a newfound respect, a tacit acknowledgement of his leadership and his unwavering commitment to the pack. She participated actively in the pack's governance, her sharp intellect and strategic thinking proving invaluable. Damian knew her loyalty was not simply earned; it was a testament to the trust they had painstakingly built together, a bond forged in shared trials and mutual respect.

The mentorship program, a cornerstone of Damian's efforts to rebuild the pack, flourished. Older wolves, seasoned veterans of countless battles, shared their wisdom and experience with the younger generation, nurturing a sense of belonging and continuity. The bonds formed were more than just mentor-mentee relationships; they were familial, strengthening the pack's fabric and solidifying its foundation. The program's success was evident in the increased confidence and camaraderie among the pack members, young and old alike.

The community garden, more than just a source of sustenance, had become a symbol of growth and renewal. Wolves, regardless of rank or status, worked side-by-side, their hands in the soil, cultivating not only food but also a shared sense of purpose. The garden represented the pack's collective effort, their unwavering commitment to rebuilding their lives and creating a thriving future for themselves and their descendants. The vibrant colors of the blossoming plants and the rich scent of fertile earth filled the air, a symphony of renewal that resonated throughout the sanctuary.

The economic recovery was slow, but steady. Damian, with the assistance of astute pack members, implemented sustainable practices, fostering economic independence and self-sufficiency. They developed new trade relationships with neighboring communities, exchanging goods and services, strengthening alliances and fostering mutual understanding. The sanctuary, once isolated and vulnerable, was now part of a wider network, a vital member of a thriving community. The prosperity was not simply material; it was a testament to their collective strength and their ability to overcome adversity.

However, the peace was not without its challenges. Whispers of dissent still circulated in the shadows, remnants of Keegan's insidious influence. Damian, always vigilant, addressed these concerns with a combination of diplomacy and decisive action. He distinguished between genuine grievances and calculated acts of subversion, offering support to those genuinely struggling while firmly dealing with those who sought to exploit the pack's vulnerabilities. Justice was swift and fair, ensuring accountability while emphasizing restorative justice.

The threat of external forces remained. Keegan's allies, scattered but not defeated, continued to pose a latent danger. Damian strengthened the pack's defenses, implementing new security measures and establishing a network of informants. He maintained a state of readiness, aware that the hard-won peace could be easily shattered. But this vigilance did not breed fear; it fueled a renewed determination, a resolve tempered by the lessons learned from the past. The pack was prepared; they were ready to defend their hard-earned peace.

Damian himself had changed. The weight of leadership had etched lines of responsibility onto his face, yet his eyes shone with a deeper understanding, a quiet resolve that inspired unwavering loyalty. His scars, both physical and emotional, served as constant reminders of the battles fought and won. He was a testament to the pack's resilience, a symbol of their shared journey through darkness and into the light. His leadership was not based on fear or intimidation, but on empathy, compassion, and unwavering determination.

The dawn of this new era was not a triumphant finale; it was a beginning. The wolves of the sanctuary had survived their darkest hour, emerging stronger and more united. Their path forward would not be without its obstacles; the shadows of the past would linger. Yet, under Damian's wise and compassionate leadership, they faced the future with hope, their collective spirit strengthened by the shared experience of struggle and triumph. A new era had begun, an era of peace, prosperity, and unwavering unity. The legacy of Keegan's tyranny was fading, replaced by the vibrant promise of a future built on hope, resilience, and the indomitable spirit of the wolf. The future was unwritten, but the wolves of the sanctuary were ready to face it, together.

Chapter 5:
Emerging Threats

The rhythmic howl of a lone wolf, piercing the stillness of the night, sent a shiver down Elara's spine. It wasn't the mournful cry of a lost pup, nor the defiant challenge of a rival pack. This howl held a different tone – a low, guttural sound that resonated deep within her bones, a primal fear that stirred ancient instincts. She glanced towards Damian, his silhouette sharp against the flickering firelight in the community hall. He hadn't reacted, yet the subtle tension in his posture mirrored her own unease.

That night, the whispers began. They weren't the usual murmurs of discontent or gossip that often slithered through the pack. These were different, carried on the wind, spoken in hushed tones, laced with a sense of dread that went beyond the lingering fear of Keegan's legacy. Tales of strange occurrences in the bordering territories – livestock vanishing without a trace, unsettling disturbances in the natural order, unsettling sightings in the shadowed corners of the ancient forests.

Initially, Damian dismissed them as superstitious ramblings, remnants of Keegan's reign of terror. He had worked tirelessly to foster a sense of security and hope within the pack, and he wasn't about to let fear, born from unfounded rumors, undermine his efforts. But the frequency of these whispers, the intensity of the fear they evoked, even within the usually stoic elders, gnawed at his composure. He found himself questioning his own certainty, a disquieting feeling he hadn't experienced since the days of Keegan's brutal rule.

One evening, an old shaman, his face etched with the wisdom and weariness of countless winters, approached Damian. His eyes, usually bright and playful, were clouded with a deep, unsettling concern. He spoke of ancient prophecies, of a slumbering evil, an entity of immense power that lay dormant beneath the earth, waiting for its time to rise.

"The whispers are true, Alpha," the shaman rasped, his voice trembling slightly. "They are not mere tales of Keegan's henchmen; they are echoes of something far older, far more sinister. A darkness stirs beneath our land, Damian. A darkness that threatens not just our pack, but the very balance of the world."

The shaman's words struck Damian like a physical blow. He had faced down Keegan, dealt with the internal divisions within the pack, and secured their fragile peace. But this...this was different. This was a threat that transcended the confines of his leadership, a threat that reached into the very fabric of existence. He pressed the shaman for details, eager to understand the nature of this "slumbering evil," but the old wolf was hesitant. The knowledge, he claimed, was too dangerous, too powerful, to be shared lightly.

Over the next few days, Damian delved into the pack's archives, searching for any mention of this ancient threat. The old texts, filled with cryptic symbols and archaic language, spoke of a primordial entity, a being of immense power that had once been imprisoned beneath the earth. Its release, the texts warned, would bring about an age of darkness, an era of unparalleled destruction. He found references to rituals, to artifacts that held the key to containing this ancient evil. The more he learned, the more he realized that Keegan's threat, however significant, had been but a minor distraction, a prelude to a far greater, more ancient evil.

The discovery of an ancient map, hidden within a secret compartment of a forgotten shrine, further solidified his fears. The map depicted a network of subterranean tunnels, a labyrinthine network leading to a hidden chamber deep beneath the earth. The chamber, according to the map's cryptic annotations, held the entity's prison, a location long forgotten by all but a select few.

Elara, ever vigilant, observed Damian's growing unease. She sensed the weight of this new threat, the burden he carried upon his shoulders. Her own unease had transformed into a grim determination. She understood the magnitude of the looming danger; the survival of the pack, indeed, the survival of the entire region, rested upon their shoulders. She offered him unwavering support, her sharp intellect proving invaluable in deciphering the ancient texts and interpreting the map's intricate details.

Together, they began to assemble a small, select team of the pack's most trusted and skilled warriors. They included Kael, a veteran warrior with unmatched combat skills and an unwavering loyalty, and Lyra, a young but exceptionally gifted healer, whose intuitive understanding of the natural world proved surprisingly relevant to the ancient lore. Their mission: to venture into the subterranean tunnels, to find the hidden chamber and assess the threat posed by the ancient evil. The journey would be treacherous, the dangers unknown, but they knew that inaction was not an option. The whispers had become a deafening roar, a warning they could no longer ignore.

The preparation for this mission was unlike anything the pack had undertaken before. They sought out forgotten rituals, studied ancient texts, and gathered rare herbs and artifacts, all in preparation for confronting an enemy beyond their comprehension. The air crackled with anticipation, a mixture of dread and grim determination. The once vibrant sanctuary was now cloaked in a palpable sense of foreboding, the laughter and music replaced by a somber quietude. Even the usually playful pups seemed to sense the impending danger, their playful barks replaced by a subdued whimper.

As they prepared to embark on their perilous journey, a chilling realization struck Damian. The ancient evil wasn't merely a threat to their pack, it was a threat to everything they had fought to build. It was a threat to the fragile peace they had achieved, to the hope that had begun to blossom within the hearts of his pack. He knew that the coming battle would not be merely a fight for survival, but a struggle for the very soul of their world. The whispers of the greater evil were no longer just whispers; they were a deafening roar, a symphony of impending doom that resonated through the very fabric of their existence. The fate of their pack, and perhaps the world, hung precariously in the balance. And as they prepared to descend into the darkness, the weight of that responsibility pressed down upon them, heavy and inescapable. This was a fight they had to win. Not just for themselves, but for generations to come.

The victory over Keegan, initially celebrated with unrestrained joy, now cast a long, unsettling shadow. The brutal purge had left wounds that ran deeper than physical scars. The pack, though outwardly unified, was fractured. Whispers of dissent, previously muted by the fear of Keegan's iron fist, now surfaced, fueled by resentment and distrust. Some questioned Damian's methods, his ruthless efficiency in eliminating Keegan's followers, seeing echoes of the very tyranny they had overthrown. Others felt abandoned, their losses still raw, their pleas for justice unheeded amidst the rush to secure the pack's immediate safety.

Kael, ever loyal, noticed the subtle shifts in the pack's dynamic. His gruff demeanor, usually a mask for his deep-seated empathy, hid a growing concern. He'd seen firsthand the brutality of Keegan's reign, the fear it instilled, the divisions it created. Yet, the methods used to dismantle it, while necessary, had inadvertently sown the seeds of new conflicts. He voiced his concerns to Damian, his words laced with caution, not criticism.

"Alpha," Kael began, his voice low and grave, "the whispers aren't just about the ancient evil. They're about us. About the choices we made, the sacrifices we demanded."

Damian, weary from the endless nights spent poring over ancient texts and strategizing for the impending threat, acknowledged Kael's words with a heavy sigh. He knew Kael was right. The victory had come at a cost. The quick, decisive actions necessary to neutralize Keegan's threat had alienated some within the pack, leaving a lingering bitterness that threatened to fester.

Lyra, her keen observations often overlooked in favor of more overtly aggressive strategies, noticed a different kind of consequence. The use of powerful, potent herbs and rituals during the final confrontation with Keegan had inadvertently disrupted the natural balance of the land. The once vibrant forests now showed signs of decay, the rivers ran slower, and the animals seemed restless, their behavior unpredictable.

"The land remembers, Alpha," Lyra whispered, her voice filled with a haunting solemnity. "Our victory has wounded the earth as well as the pack." She showed Damian faded, almost imperceptible marks on the ancient trees – strange symbols that mirrored those found in the texts detailing the ancient evil's imprisonment. These weren't simply natural markings; they were signs of a deeper, more insidious imbalance.

The unexpected consequences extended beyond the immediate pack. Neighboring packs, previously hesitant to engage with the now-liberated pack, held back, wary of the newly established order. Rumors of Damian's ruthlessness spread like wildfire, casting doubt on his ability to lead not only his own pack but also to foster peaceful relations with others. This isolation threatened to leave them vulnerable, a severe disadvantage as they braced themselves for the ancient evil's awakening.

The weight of these unforeseen consequences pressed heavily on Damian. He grappled with the realization that leadership wasn't just about strength and decisiveness; it was about empathy, understanding, and the ability to navigate the complex web of human – or rather, wolf – emotions and consequences. He'd been so focused on defeating Keegan that he hadn't fully considered the ripple effects of his actions, the lingering trauma, the resentment, the fractured trust.

He summoned the pack elders, the most experienced and respected members, for a council. The meeting was tense, each wolf carrying the weight of their past experiences and present anxieties. The discussion was far from easy. Old wounds were reopened, long-held resentments voiced. Damian listened patiently, allowing the elders to express their concerns and frustrations without interruption. He admitted his shortcomings, acknowledging the unintended consequences of his actions. It was a humbling experience, a stark reminder that even the most well-intentioned actions can have devastating unforeseen repercussions.

Elara, ever the strategist, saw an opportunity within this challenge. She proposed a plan to mend the rifts within the pack, a plan that involved open dialogues, collective healing rituals, and a renewed emphasis on community building. She suggested incorporating traditional methods of conflict resolution, using ancient practices to address the emotional wounds and foster reconciliation.

The healing process was slow and arduous, requiring patience, understanding, and a willingness to confront the painful truths of their recent past. The pack underwent a period of introspection, a time of healing and reconciliation. They held community ceremonies, sharing stories, expressing their grief, and collectively working to overcome their internal divisions.

The process was far from perfect. Old resentments lingered, trust was rebuilt slowly, brick by agonizing brick. But the effort, the willingness to confront their internal conflicts, proved crucial. The pack, though scarred, began to heal, its unity strengthened through the shared experience of confronting their past mistakes and working towards a more balanced future.

The challenges, however, didn't end there. As they prepared for their descent into the subterranean tunnels, a new threat emerged – a faction of Keegan's surviving followers, embittered and vengeful, seeking to exploit the pack's internal divisions. Led by a cunning and ruthless lieutenant named Roric, this faction used the pack's vulnerabilities to their advantage, stirring unrest and sowing chaos. Their attacks were subtle, aimed at undermining Damian's authority and sowing discord. They were a constant, nagging reminder of the lingering consequences of their past actions, a new obstacle in their already perilous journey.

Damian realized that the fight for the pack's survival was not solely against the ancient evil slumbering beneath the earth; it was also against the insidious forces of internal conflict and external aggression. This two-pronged threat pushed them to their limits, testing their resilience and strength in ways they had never imagined. The weight of responsibility, once borne alone by Damian, was now shared, a collective burden carried by a pack slowly but surely rediscovering its unity and strength. The journey to the hidden chamber was no longer just a quest to confront an ancient evil; it had become a testament to their enduring spirit, a demonstration of their capacity for resilience and their unwavering commitment to their survival, both individually and as a pack. The unforeseen consequences of the past had created new, unexpected challenges, but from the ashes of those challenges, a stronger, more resilient pack was beginning to rise. The road ahead remained treacherous, but they were ready to face it, together.

The air hung heavy with the scent of pine and damp earth, a stark contrast to the acrid smell of burnt fur and fear that had permeated the pack's territory just weeks ago. The healing process, though underway, was far from complete. The scars, both physical and emotional, remained. Yet, a fragile peace had settled over the pack, a fragile truce born from shared grief and the arduous work of reconciliation. Damian, observing the tentative rebuilding of unity, felt a flicker of hope, a spark in the suffocating darkness of their impending confrontation with the ancient evil.

But the respite was short-lived. Roric's insidious attacks continued, a relentless barrage of subtle sabotage and calculated disinformation designed to fracture the pack from within. He preyed on existing wounds, fanning the embers of resentment into raging flames. Damian knew he needed more than just internal healing; he needed external support, a strategic alliance to counter Roric's machinations and prepare for the far greater threat below.

His gaze fell upon an ancient, weathered map, detailing the hidden pathways and forgotten settlements of the surrounding lands. One marking, a faded symbol he'd never encountered before, caught his attention. It resembled a stylized serpent coiled around a blazing sun, a symbol of power and ancient magic that resonated with a strange familiarity. Lyra, upon seeing it, gasped.

"The Solarii," she whispered, her voice barely above a murmur. "A group of sun mages, protectors of the ancient balance. They live secluded in the Whispering Mountains, rarely interacting with the outside world. Their magic is... unique, unlike anything we've encountered before."

The Solarii. The very name sparked a debate among the elders. Some warned of their aloofness, their distrust of outsiders, particularly those associated with the wolf packs. Others spoke of their immense power, their deep connection to the earth and its energies, a power that could potentially tip the balance in their favor. Damian, recognizing the desperate need for allies, decided to take the risk.

The journey to the Whispering Mountains was arduous, a test of endurance and resilience. The terrain was unforgiving, the weather unpredictable, but the pack persevered, driven by the urgency of their situation and the hope of finding a powerful ally. They finally reached a hidden valley, shrouded in mist and bathed in the ethereal glow of the setting sun. There, amidst ancient, towering pines, stood a village unlike any they had ever seen – homes carved directly into the rock face, adorned with intricate sun-shaped symbols, the air vibrating with potent, yet calming, energy.

The Solarii welcomed them with a mixture of curiosity and caution. Their leader, a woman named Anya, her eyes as bright and intense as the sun itself, observed Damian and his pack with a sharp, discerning gaze. She possessed an aura of quiet strength, her every movement imbued with a graceful power that spoke of years spent honing her abilities. The initial encounter was fraught with tension, a careful dance of suspicion and mutual respect.

Anya, speaking in a melodious voice that resonated with the warmth of the sun, explained that the Solarii were guardians of the earth's delicate balance, protectors of the natural world against forces that threatened its equilibrium. She listened patiently as Damian recounted their struggle against Keegan and the emerging threat of the ancient evil, his voice resonating with the weight of his responsibility. She spoke of the imbalance caused by the powerful herbs and rituals used in the fight against Keegan, confirming Lyra's observations.

"The land bleeds, Alpha Damian," Anya stated, her voice carrying the weight of centuries of wisdom. "Your victory has created a wound, a disruption in the natural order. The ancient evil senses this weakness, this imbalance. It feeds on chaos, on disharmony." Her words were a chilling confirmation of their worst fears.

The alliance wasn't formed overnight. There were significant cultural differences to navigate, fundamental distinctions in their approach to magic and conflict resolution. The Solarii's emphasis on harmony and balance contrasted sharply with the wolf pack's more aggressive, instinctual tactics. Discussions were long and intense, often punctuated by moments of friction. The Solarii initially questioned Damian's methods, his ruthless efficiency in eliminating Keegan's followers. The brutality, while necessary, was antithetical to their philosophy of peaceful coexistence.

Damian, humbled by their criticisms, made an effort to understand their perspective, to find common ground. He acknowledged the shortcomings of his past actions, the unintended consequences that had shaken the foundations of his pack. He shared his vision for a future where the wolf pack and the Solarii could coexist, their strengths complementing each other, their combined powers formidable enough to confront the ancient evil.

The turning point arrived during a shared healing ritual. The Solarii performed a ceremony that drew upon the earth's energy to mend the wounds inflicted upon the land, using intricate chants and mesmerizing movements that seemed to resonate with the very fabric of reality. The ceremony was not just about healing the physical landscape; it was about restoring balance, re-harmonizing the disrupted energies. The wolves participated, their inherent connection to nature amplifying the ritual's effect. It was during this ceremony that a genuine understanding began to bloom, a shared empathy born from a mutual respect for the land and its delicate equilibrium.

The alliance, once precarious and uncertain, solidified. Anya, recognizing Damian's genuine remorse and his willingness to learn, agreed to aid the pack in their quest. She offered the Solarii's unique magic – their ability to manipulate solar energy – as a powerful weapon against the ancient evil. They would work together, combining their distinct strengths to overcome the formidable challenges ahead.

The combined knowledge of the wolf pack and the Solarii proved invaluable. The Solarii's understanding of the land's energies allowed them to identify weaknesses in the ancient evil's defenses, pathways that remained hidden to the wolf pack. They revealed hidden passages and ancient tunnels, circumventing the more heavily guarded routes. The Solarii also shared ancient protective wards and rituals, strengthening the pack's defenses against Roric's relentless attacks.

The alliance was not without its challenges. The contrasting approaches to strategy and conflict resolution created new tensions. The Solarii's preference for non-violent solutions often clashed with the wolf pack's more aggressive tactics. Damian had to navigate these differences, fostering cooperation while respecting the unique strengths of each group. He learned to balance the Solarii's emphasis on harmony with the wolf pack's inherent need for decisive action.

The partnership, however, was proving to be stronger than its challenges. The combined knowledge and skills of the two groups proved invaluable in their preparations for the descent into the subterranean tunnels. They were a united front, a force to be reckoned with, ready to face whatever awaited them beneath the earth. The unexpected alliance forged in the crucible of shared adversity had not only strengthened their resolve but had also deepened their understanding of the intricate web of life, demonstrating the power of cooperation and the importance of respect for diverse perspectives in the face of overwhelming odds. The path ahead remained shrouded in darkness, but the combined light of the sun mages and the wolf pack shone brighter, illuminating a path towards hope, however uncertain that path might be.

The valley, nestled deep within the Whispering Mountains, hummed with a quiet energy, a tangible thrumming that vibrated beneath the soles of the wolves' paws. The Solarii, with their sun-kissed skin and eyes that mirrored the celestial fire, moved with a grace that belied their immense power. They were not warriors in the traditional sense, but their mastery of solar energy translated into a different kind of strength—a strength that could mend the earth and shatter stone with equal ease.

Damian, his wolfish features etched with the weight of responsibility, oversaw the preparations. Anya, the Solarii leader, stood beside him, her calm demeanor a stark contrast to the nervous energy radiating from the assembled pack. Their combined knowledge was being meticulously cataloged, a tapestry woven from centuries of experience and the urgent need for survival.

The maps, meticulously drawn and annotated by the Solarii, were spread out on large, flat stones. They depicted not just the terrain, but the flow of energy beneath the surface, the ley lines that pulsed with raw power, and the points of vulnerability in the ancient evil's subterranean realm. The wolves' intimate knowledge of the surrounding forests, honed over generations, complemented the Solarii's insightful understanding of the earth's subtle energies. They were building a three-dimensional map of the enemy's territory, one that wasn't confined to geographical coordinates but extended into the mystical realm of energy flows.

Lyra, her keen intellect as sharp as her senses, focused on translating the Solarii's ancient texts and symbols. These texts detailed the rituals and defenses of the ancient evil, revealing patterns and weaknesses that could be exploited. Her work was crucial, bridging the gap between the Solarii's arcane knowledge and the pack's practical understanding of combat strategy. The translations revealed ancient incantations, protective wards, and the very essence of the being they were about to confront. This wasn't a brute force encounter; it was a battle of wits, a test of knowledge and magical prowess.

The Solarii's understanding of protective wards proved particularly valuable. They taught the wolves how to weave protective shields using solar energy, a countermeasure against the psychic attacks and manipulative illusions the ancient evil was known to employ. They demonstrated how to channel the sun's power to create barriers that were impenetrable to even the most potent dark magic. The wolves, accustomed to relying on their physical strength and pack cohesion, found this newfound ability both exhilarating and empowering. It broadened their strategic horizons, granting them abilities they hadn't previously imagined.

Meanwhile, the pack's warriors underwent rigorous training, honing their skills and coordinating their movements with the precision of a finely tuned machine. Damian pushed them to their limits, demanding unwavering focus and discipline. He knew the battle ahead would be unlike any they had faced before. This wasn't just about strength; it was about strategy, coordination, and a deep understanding of the enemy's capabilities. The training sessions were brutal, but the wolves responded with unmatched dedication, their shared purpose forging an unbreakable bond.

The preparation also involved the creation of specialized weaponry. The Solarii, using their mastery over solar energy, forged weapons infused with sun-fire—daggers that glowed with blinding radiance and spears that crackled with potent energy. These weapons were designed to combat the ancient evil's dark magic, to burn away its shadowy tendrils and disrupt its power. They were imbued with runes and symbols from the Solarii texts, enhancing their capabilities and aligning them with the forces of light.

Beyond the physical preparations, there was a more profound level of strategizing. Damian, guided by Anya's wisdom and Lyra's knowledge, devised a complex plan that incorporated both the Solarii's magical abilities and the wolf pack's fighting prowess. They identified multiple points of entry into the ancient evil's lair, each tailored to different strategies and tactics. The approach was multifaceted, designed to disrupt the enemy's defenses and catch it off guard.

One strategy involved a diversionary tactic. A small group of wolves, aided by Solarii wards and illusions, would create a diversion at a heavily guarded entrance while the main force launched a surprise attack through a less-defended passage identified by the Solarii using their unique understanding of the land's energetic currents. The plan incorporated elements of deception and misdirection, designed to exploit the ancient evil's blind spots and its over-reliance on its own formidable defenses.

The Solarii's unique approach to healing also played a vital role in the preparations. They conducted a series of rituals designed to fortify the wolf pack, enhancing their natural abilities and bolstering their resilience against the dark magic they would encounter. These rituals were not merely about physical healing; they strengthened the wolves' spiritual resolve, creating a powerful inner resilience that would prove invaluable against the psychological warfare tactics of their opponent.

The days leading up to the confrontation were filled with a palpable tension, a mixture of anticipation and apprehension. The wolves, usually boisterous and playful, moved with a quiet intensity, their eyes focused and determined. The Solarii, typically serene and contemplative, radiated a quiet strength, their energy humming with anticipation. Even the air seemed to hold its breath, charged with the weight of the looming conflict.

In the heart of their preparations, Damian found himself wrestling with an internal conflict. He had come to admire the Solarii's approach to conflict resolution—their emphasis on harmony and peaceful coexistence. This contrasted sharply with his own ruthless efficiency, the pragmatism born out of necessity in his fight for survival. He recognized the need to temper his aggressive instincts with the Solarii's emphasis on balance, acknowledging that true victory lay not just in defeating the enemy but also in preserving the delicate harmony of the natural world.

The final preparations included a solemn ceremony. Under the watchful eyes of the setting sun, the wolves and the Solarii gathered, their combined energies intertwining in a powerful ritual. It was a pledge of unity, a shared commitment to face the approaching threat together. They stood as one, a powerful force united by a common purpose, their combined strengths poised to shatter the ancient darkness that threatened their world. The air crackled with anticipation, the silence broken only by the rustling of the pines and the quiet determination echoing in their hearts. They were ready. The time for action was at hand.

The final preparations completed, a sense of uneasy calm settled over the valley. The air, once thick with the nervous energy of anticipation, now held a different weight – the heavy silence before a storm. Damian, his wolfish gaze sweeping across the assembled warriors, felt a familiar knot tighten in his stomach. This wasn't the familiar threat of rival packs or territorial disputes. This was something far older, far more insidious. Something that resonated with a primal fear deep within his very bones.

Anya, ever the pragmatist, broke the silence. "The tremors have increased," she stated, her voice calm yet firm, her sun-kissed skin seeming to absorb the last vestiges of daylight. "The ancient one stirs."

Lyra, her eyes still shadowed with fatigue from her tireless work deciphering ancient texts, nodded in grim agreement. "The prophecies spoke of a gathering storm, a convergence of darkness that would herald its true power. It seems that time has come." She held up a worn, leather-bound book, its pages filled with cryptic symbols and faded ink. "The texts hint at a power beyond anything we have encountered. A power that transcends the boundaries of the physical world, drawing strength from the very fabric of existence."

The words hung in the air, heavy with foreboding. The wolves, hardened by years of survival, exchanged apprehensive glances. Even the Solarii, masters of solar energy and unwavering in their faith, showed a flicker of uncertainty in their eyes. The ancient one was not merely a powerful being; it was an entity that drew strength from despair, feeding on fear and chaos.

The first signs of the approaching threat weren't violent, but subtle. A chilling wind swept through the valley, carrying with it a whisper of dread, a phantom touch that raised goosebumps on even the thickest fur. The usually vibrant colors of the valley seemed muted, dulled by an encroaching darkness. The sun, which had been a constant source of strength and warmth for the Solarii, seemed to lose its brilliance, its light dimmed by an unseen force.

Then came the tremors. Not the gentle earth movements they had grown accustomed to, but violent shudders that rattled the very foundations of the mountains. The ground groaned beneath their paws, cracks appearing in the earth, fissures that spewed forth a dark, viscous substance that hissed and bubbled like something unholy.

The air itself crackled with a sinister energy, a tangible malevolence that pressed down upon them, a suffocating blanket of dread. The wolves instinctively bared their fangs, their fur bristling with primal fear. Even the usually calm Solarii drew upon their solar energy, their bodies glowing faintly as they created protective shields around themselves and the pack.

As the darkness intensified, strange, unsettling visions began to plague the wolves. Whispers slithered into their minds, insidious suggestions that played on their deepest fears and insecurities.

They saw fragmented images of loved ones falling victim to unspeakable horrors, images so vivid and real that they felt the icy grip of despair clawing at their hearts. This was the ancient one's prelude, a psychic assault designed to break their spirits before the physical confrontation.

Damian, however, held firm. Remembering the Solarii's teachings, he focused on the sun's warmth, on the strength of his pack, and on the shared purpose that bound them together. He urged his warriors to do the same, reminding them of the training, the rituals, and the unwavering belief in their cause. The visions persisted, but their power diminished as the wolves collectively resisted, their unified minds forming a bulwark against the ancient one's psychic assault.

Lyra, meanwhile, tirelessly worked to identify the source of the growing darkness. Using her knowledge of ancient languages and the Solarii's maps, she traced the energetic signatures of the encroaching evil, trying to pinpoint its location and predict its next move. The texts suggested that the ancient one drew strength from a nexus of dark energy located deep beneath the earth, a point of convergence where the veil between worlds thinned, allowing it to draw power from realms beyond human comprehension.

As the night deepened, the tremors grew more frequent and more intense. The ground buckled and cracked, creating chasms that swallowed entire trees and sent rocks hurtling into the air. The dark, viscous substance seeped forth in greater quantities, forming a slowly spreading pool that pulsed with an ominous, malevolent energy. The air crackled with unseen power, charged with a tangible sense of dread.

The whispers intensified, weaving elaborate tales of impending doom, of inevitable defeat. They were meant to break the wolves' resolve, to sow discord amongst the ranks and weaken their defenses. But the warriors, strengthened by the Solarii's rituals and Damian's unwavering leadership, stood firm. Their determination was not shaken.

Amid the chaos, a new, horrifying sound began to penetrate the air - a deep, guttural growl that resonated with the very earth itself. It was a sound that spoke of immense power, of ancient malevolence, a sound that chilled them to the very core. The ancient one was revealing its true strength, its presence growing more imposing, more terrifying with every passing moment.

The sky above, once clear, now swirled with dark clouds, obscuring the moon and stars. A suffocating darkness descended, a palpable manifestation of the ancient one's encroaching power. The air itself seemed to vibrate with a malevolent energy, the ground trembling under the weight of its wrath. This was the prelude to the storm – a maelstrom of darkness that promised to engulf them all. The true battle was about to begin. The gathering storm had arrived, bringing with it an ancient evil that threatened to consume their world. The weight of their impending confrontation was nearly unbearable. Their training, their strategy, their unity— it all hinged on this moment. The time for preparation was over. The time for action was now.

Chapter 6:
Final Confrontation

The guttural growl reverberated through their very bones, a prelude to the cataclysm that was about to unfold. From the heart of the encroaching darkness, a colossal figure emerged, its form shifting and swirling like smoke, yet impossibly solid. It was a grotesque parody of nature, a monstrous amalgamation of shadow and twisted flesh, its eyes burning with malevolent energy. The ancient one had revealed itself.

Damian, drawing on years of honed instincts and the unwavering strength of the Solarii's teachings, roared a command. The wolves, a unified force, charged forward, their teeth bared, their eyes blazing with a fierce determination that mirrored his own. Anya, her sun-kissed skin radiating with an ethereal glow, unleashed a torrent of solar energy, blinding bolts of light that struck the ancient one's form, momentarily disrupting its monstrous shape.

The battle began as a furious maelstrom of claw and fang, of solar energy and shadow magic. The wolves, utilizing their superior agility and pack tactics, swarmed the ancient one, their bites and scratches doing surprisingly little to harm its formidable form. But they held it, keeping it occupied, giving the Solarii time to unleash their devastating attacks. Lyra, despite the exhaustion etched upon her face, remained steadfast, channeling the ancient texts into protective wards, bolstering the wolves' defenses and disrupting the ancient one's malevolent energy. Her voice, laced with power drawn from the ages, guided their movements, correcting their stances and improving their attacks. She was the conductor of their orchestra, ensuring harmony and synergy.

The ancient one responded with a wave of pure darkness, a tide of suffocating gloom that threatened to extinguish the Solarii's light. The wolves were thrown back, their bodies shuddering under the impact. But they regrouped, their loyalty and resolve unwavering. Damian, his wolfish instincts sharpened by the fight, leaped forward, his teeth sinking into the ancient one's shadowy flesh, only to find his fangs meeting an unnatural resistance, a chilling cold that seemed to drain the warmth from his very soul.

The ancient one retaliated with a psychic attack of unimaginable intensity, a deluge of terrifying visions that sought to break their wills. The wolves staggered, their minds reeling under the onslaught of horrifying images – their loved ones tormented, their homes destroyed, their world consumed by darkness. But Damian, drawing upon the strength of his pack, focused on their shared purpose. He reminded them of the lives they were defending and the future they were fighting for. He held them together with the power of his will and the strength of their bond.

Anya, sensing their faltering resolve, poured more solar energy into the fight. She didn't just attack the ancient one but also focused her light on her allies, bathing them in a protective glow that shielded them from the psychic assault. The wolves, bolstered by her light, regained their footing. They held their heads high, their resolve strengthened and unwavering.

The battle raged on, an epic clash between light and darkness, between hope and despair. The ground trembled, the air crackled, and the very fabric of reality seemed to tear under the strain of their conflict. The wolves fought with a ferocity born of desperation, their fangs and claws tearing into the ancient one's shadowy form, inflicting small wounds that, surprisingly, seemed to have an effect.

Lyra, her brow slick with sweat, deciphered a hidden passage in the ancient texts. A secret ritual, a forgotten technique that could potentially disrupt the ancient one's connection to the nexus of dark energy. She relayed the instructions to Damian, her voice strained but clear. Damian, adapting his fighting style, focused his attacks on the spots that Lyra's texts revealed to be the creature's vulnerable points.

The ancient one's roars echoed through the valley, its fury growing with each passing moment. Its power was immense, capable of tearing apart the very mountains, yet the wolves and Solarii refused to yield. They fought not just for their survival, but for the future of their world. They fought for the light.

The climax arrived with a surge of power from both sides. Damian, channeling all his strength and rage, launched a devastating attack, using Lyra's newly discovered knowledge to strike at the ancient one's core, disrupting its connection to the dark nexus that fed its power. Simultaneously, Anya unleashed a blinding wave of solar energy, a magnificent eruption of light that washed over the battlefield. The ancient one shrieked, its form dissolving as the light overwhelmed it.

The darkness receded, the tremors subsided, and the ground stopped its agonizing groans. The oppressive weight of the ancient one's presence lifted, replaced by a sense of relief so profound it was almost painful. The victory was hard-won, brutal and costly, but a victory nonetheless. The wolves were exhausted, their bodies battered and scarred, but their spirits remained unbroken.

The battleground was a desolate wasteland, a testament to the ferocity of the conflict. The stench of burning earth and shattered shadow clung to the air. But amid the ruins, a glimmer of hope remained. The sun peeked through the dissipating clouds, casting a warm glow upon the exhausted warriors. The world had been saved, at least for now. The final confrontation was over, but the journey of healing had just begun. The scars of the battle would remain, both physical and emotional, but they would stand as a reminder of their resilience and their unity, a beacon of hope in a world forever changed. The wolves, battered but unbroken, huddled together, sharing a quiet moment of victory before the arduous task of rebuilding their lives and their world began. The echoes of the epic battle would forever reverberate through the valley, a legend whispered through generations to come.

The ancient one's demise wasn't clean. Even as its shadowy form dissolved, tendrils of darkness snaked out, desperately clinging to the fading light. One such tendril, thick as a pythons, lashed out with surprising speed, catching Damian squarely in the chest. He cried out, a raw, animal sound that tore through the silence of the aftermath, a sound that was almost instantly swallowed by the triumphant howling of the wolves.

Anya screamed, her radiant glow momentarily flickering as she rushed to his side. Lyra, her face etched with both relief and horror, scrambled to his aid, her hands moving over his chest, muttering incantations in a desperate attempt to stanch the flow of dark energy. The dark energy, unlike any they had encountered before, was seeping into him, a chilling cold that seemed to freeze his very soul. His body, once vibrantly alive, now seemed to be slowly fading, the light of life draining from his eyes.

The wolves, their earlier jubilation extinguished, gathered around him, their whimpers a mournful chorus echoing the anguish in Anya and Lyra's hearts. They nudged him gently, their muzzles resting against his bloodied form, a silent testament to their unwavering loyalty and their despair. The victory they had fought so hard for felt hollow, overshadowed by the looming specter of Damian's impending death.

The dark energy was insidious, a creeping corruption that threatened to consume him entirely. Anya's solar energy, while potent, seemed powerless against this particular brand of darkness. It was a relentless drain, sapping his life force, leaving him pale and weak, his breathing shallow and ragged. Lyra frantically searched through the ancient texts, hoping to find a counter-spell, a solution to this unforeseen tragedy. The texts, however, offered no easy answers. This was a new kind of magic, more powerful and insidious than anything they had faced before.

The silence was broken only by Damian's ragged breaths and the soft whimpers of the wolves. He opened his eyes, his gaze flickering across the faces of his companions, his expression a mixture of pain and serene acceptance. He reached out a trembling hand, touching Anya's cheek. His touch, once warm and strong, was now icy cold.

"Don't...don't mourn me," he whispered, his voice barely audible. "We...we won. The world is safe... for now."

Anya sobbed, unable to speak, her tears falling onto his hand. She desperately wanted to deny the reality of his fading life, to somehow reverse the creeping darkness that was consuming him. She knew it was hopeless, but she couldn't bring herself to accept it.

Lyra, despite her own grief, remained focused. She continued to pour over the ancient texts, desperately seeking a solution. She knew that the ancient one's power had been tied to a dark nexus, and this dark energy was possibly a lingering fragment of that nexus, clinging onto Damian as a last act of vengeance. She had to find a way to sever that connection.

Hours bled into each other, the sun slowly setting, casting long shadows over the desolate battlefield. Damian's life ebbed away, his body growing colder and stiller. His grip on Anya's hand loosened, and his eyes fluttered closed. For a moment, a terrible silence hung in the air, the silence of loss and grief. Then, a faint, almost imperceptible flicker of light emanated from Damian's chest, a small, defiant spark in the face of encroaching darkness.

Lyra gasped, her eyes widening in disbelief. She had found it—a hidden passage in the ancient texts, a ritual of sacrifice and redemption. It was a dangerous ritual, one that required a tremendous amount of energy and could potentially consume the person performing it. But it was their only hope. She explained the ritual to Anya, her voice trembling with a mixture of fear and hope. Anya, her grief momentarily pushed aside by the urgency of the situation, nodded resolutely.

The ritual required a conduit—a vessel through which the dark energy could be channeled and dispelled. Damian, even in his deathly state, was still connected to the dark energy that had wounded him. His body was the vessel. Anya, fueled by her immense solar energy and her undying love for Damian, would be the one to perform the ritual. It was a gamble, a desperate attempt to save him, even if it meant pushing herself to the brink of destruction.

With Lyra guiding her, Anya began the ritual. The air crackled with energy, a vibrant display of light and shadow clashing in a desperate ballet of life and death. Anya's body glowed with an intense light, her energy pouring into Damian's weakened form. She channeled the light, not just to fight the darkness but also to coax the lingering spark of life back into Damian's body. It was a grueling process, a battle fought on the edge of oblivion. Anya felt herself growing weaker with each passing moment, yet she held on, her determination fuelled by the memory of Damian and their shared dreams.

The dark energy began to recede. Slowly, the icy cold that had gripped Damian's body began to dissipate, replaced by a faint warmth. His breathing grew stronger, his pulse steadier. The colour returned to his face, a faint blush blooming on his pale cheeks. The faint flicker of light in his chest strengthened, growing into a steady flame.

Anya collapsed, her body drained of energy, but a small smile played on her lips. Damian's eyes fluttered open, his gaze meeting hers. He reached out and gently touched her face, a single tear tracing a path down his cheek. He was alive. He was alive, thanks to Anya's incredible sacrifice and the power of their love. The darkness had been banished, not only from his body but also from their hearts. The sacrifice had bought their redemption, a rebirth not just for him, but for their relationship, for their pack, and for the world they had saved. Their journey had been harrowing, their victory hard-won, their scars would remain, both physical and emotional, but they had stood together, facing the impossible, emerging victorious, united and stronger than ever.

The wolves, sensing the shift in energy, whined softly, their bodies pressing closer to Damian. Their loyalty, unwavering even in the face of death, was a balm to the aching hearts of Anya and Lyra. The air hummed with residual magic, a chaotic symphony of light and shadow still echoing the intensity of the battle. The ground, once churned and scarred by the ancient one's destructive power, seemed to sigh in relief, the very earth seemingly exhaling the weight of the conflict.

Anya, her own energy depleted to a dangerous level, slumped against a nearby rock, her breathing shallow and ragged. The luminous glow that had always surrounded her, a beacon of hope and resilience, was now a faint shimmer, a testament to the immense toll the ritual had taken. Lyra, despite her exhaustion, moved with a renewed sense of purpose. She meticulously collected the scattered remnants of the ancient one's power – shards of solidified darkness that crackled with residual energy. She knew these fragments held potential, a potential for both creation and destruction. Their careful study could lead to new defenses against future threats, a new understanding of the balance between light and shadow.

Damian stirred. A soft groan escaped his lips, followed by a slow blink of his eyes. He looked around, his gaze lingering on Anya, then Lyra, then the assembled wolves, a flicker of confusion crossing his face. The darkness that had threatened to consume him had been vanquished, but the aftereffects were still present – a deep, bone-chilling exhaustion that permeated his entire being. He attempted to raise a hand, a weak gesture of acknowledgment, but his arm trembled with weakness.

Lyra, ever the pragmatist, wasted no time in administering a potent concoction brewed from rare herbs and infused with a sliver of solar energy harvested from Anya's lingering aura. The potion, bitter and potent, burned as it flowed down his throat, but its warmth spread through him, revitalizing his body and restoring some of his lost strength. He sat up, leaning heavily on Anya for support, his eyes meeting hers.

"I... I don't remember much," Damian confessed, his voice a rough whisper, "but the darkness... it felt like... like drowning in ice. And then... light."

Anya smiled weakly, her heart overflowing with a mixture of relief and profound exhaustion. The intensity of the ritual had pushed her to the very brink of oblivion, but the sight of Damian alive, breathing, filled her with an overwhelming sense of purpose and strength. The near-death experience had only strengthened their bond, forging an unbreakable link between their souls.

Their victory, however, wasn't without its lingering questions. The ancient one's death had not been a clean severance. Lyra's initial analysis of the remaining dark fragments revealed an unsettling truth – the ancient one hadn't simply been vanquished; it had been... fragmented. Its essence, its power, had splintered into countless pieces, scattered across the land. Each fragment, though significantly weaker than the whole, held the potential to corrupt and infect. The threat was not entirely gone, merely dormant, waiting to be awakened.

The wolves, sensing the gravity of the situation, howled a mournful chorus, a chilling reminder of the fragility of their victory. Their celebration had been short-lived, replaced by a quiet apprehension. The ancient one's reign of terror was over, but the fight for their world's safety had just begun.

Lyra spent the following days painstakingly mapping the locations of these dark fragments. Using ancient cartography and a combination of magic and deduction, she identified scattered points across the land where these fragments pulsed with residual energy. Each location presented a unique challenge, requiring different approaches and strategies. The team realized that their initial victory was just the first step in a protracted campaign to secure their world's future.

The task ahead was daunting, but they approached it with a renewed sense of unity and resolve. The near-death experience had shattered any lingering doubts or uncertainties. They had faced the impossible, stared into the abyss, and emerged victorious. Their bond, tested and strengthened in the crucible of conflict, was unbreakable.

The subsequent months were a whirlwind of activity. Lyra, aided by Anya's unwavering solar energy and Damian's newfound wisdom, initiated a series of carefully planned expeditions to collect and neutralize the scattered fragments. Each encounter was a perilous dance between light and shadow, a constant battle against the insidious nature of the dark energy.

They learned to anticipate the fragments' unpredictable behavior, adapting their strategies to suit the unique properties of each. Some fragments were encased in impervious shells, demanding innovative approaches to containment. Others emitted powerful waves of dark energy that could only be countered by specific spells and rituals. Their battles tested their skills, pushing them to their limits.

Damian, once solely reliant on his physical prowess, discovered a latent affinity for magic, a hidden potential awakened by the near-death experience. Guided by Lyra, he began to harness the power of the earth, channeling its protective energies to counteract the dark magic. His transformation was remarkable, a testament to his resilience and adaptability.

Anya, having sacrificed so much during the ritual, found a new depth to her powers. Her connection to the sun, once a source of radiant energy, had now become a conduit for healing and protection. She learned to manipulate her solar energy with a level of finesse that was previously unimaginable, becoming a beacon of light and healing.

Lyra's expertise in ancient lore and magic became essential in their ongoing campaigns. She became the mastermind of their strategy, foreseeing potential dangers and adapting their plans accordingly. Her knowledge of ancient runes and rituals proved invaluable in containing and neutralizing the dark fragments.

Their journey was far from over. The task of cleansing their world from the lingering fragments of the ancient one's power was a daunting one, a constant battle against the insidious darkness. Yet, they faced the challenges with unwavering determination, their shared experiences forging an unshakeable bond that transcended the usual bounds of friendship and loyalty. Their victory was not merely a defeat of a single entity; it was the beginning of a new era, an era where they would continue to fight for their world, united and ready for whatever challenges the future may bring. The scars they bore – both physical and emotional – were a constant reminder of the battles they had won, a testament to their unwavering resilience and their undying hope. The world was safe, for now, but their vigil continued, ensuring that the darkness would not return. Their journey was far from over, and they faced it together.

The aftermath of the battle was a stark contrast to the furious chaos that had preceded it. Silence, heavy and profound, descended upon the ravaged landscape. The air, thick with the lingering scent of ozone and burnt earth, felt strangely still, a deceptive calm that masked the underlying currents of residual magic. The wolves, usually boisterous and playful, were subdued, their usual exuberance replaced by a wary stillness. They circled the trio – Anya, Lyra, and Damian – their eyes reflecting the flickering embers of the dying fire.

Damian, though revived by Lyra's potent concoction, remained weak, his body aching from the brutal fight. The darkness had left its mark, not just physically, but emotionally too. The experience had chipped away at his bravado, revealing a vulnerability he'd kept carefully hidden beneath layers of hardened self-reliance. He sat leaning against Anya, his hand instinctively seeking hers, finding comfort in her warmth. He felt a deep weariness settle over him, a weariness that went beyond mere physical exhaustion. It was a weariness of the soul, the weight of witnessing the sheer destructive power of the ancient one, the weight of almost succumbing to its chilling embrace.

Anya, her usual radiant glow dimmed, felt a similar exhaustion, but her gaze held an unwavering strength. The ritual had cost her dearly, but the sight of Damian alive fueled her spirit. The bond they shared, tested and refined in the crucible of near-death, shone brighter than ever before. She squeezed Damian's hand gently, offering a silent reassurance.

Lyra, her face etched with concentration, examined the remaining fragments of the ancient one's power. They pulsed faintly, like dying stars, emitting a faint, chilling energy. These weren't merely remnants of the ancient one's power; they were seeds of potential chaos, capable of sprouting new darkness if left unchecked. The immediate threat was vanquished, but the war was far from over. A chilling realization washed over her; this was not the end, but a new beginning. A new chapter in the ongoing battle against the encroaching shadows.

The following days were a blur of activity. Lyra, with Anya's assistance in mapping the residual energy signatures, meticulously charted the locations of these scattered fragments. The ancient texts, deciphered with Lyra's unique understanding, offered cryptic clues, leading them on a perilous chase across the land. Each fragment was a ticking time bomb, capable of unleashing pockets of darkness that could corrupt the land and its inhabitants. They weren't dealing with a single entity anymore; they were facing a diffuse threat, a creeping darkness that threatened to consume the world piece by piece.

Their first expedition led them to a desolate mountain pass, shrouded in perpetual twilight. Here, a fragment of the ancient one's power was embedded within a towering obsidian spire, pulsating with a sinister energy that chilled them to the bone. Damian, his newly discovered affinity for earth magic blossoming, channeled the earth's energy to create a protective barrier, shielding them from the fragment's corrosive aura. Anya's solar energy provided the counter-force, a radiant shield that neutralized the dark energy, slowly but surely weakening the fragment's influence. Lyra, using a combination of ancient runes and powerful incantations, sealed the fragment within a protective crystal, preventing it from further spreading its malevolent influence.

Their next target was a hidden grove, where a fragment had corrupted a sacred spring, poisoning the water and tainting the surrounding land. The challenge here was different; they had to purify the water, cleanse the land, and neutralize the fragment without destroying the sacred grove itself. Anya's healing powers were critical here, her solar energy weaving through the tainted water, slowly but surely purifying it, revitalizing the dying vegetation. Damian's earth magic stabilized the land, preventing further corruption, while Lyra devised a ritual to bind the fragment, trapping it within a protective amulet.

As they journeyed across the land, they discovered that the fragments weren't merely passive remnants of power; they reacted to their presence, responding to their emotions and intentions. The fragments seemed to feed on fear and despair, growing stronger when met with trepidation, and weakening when met with courage and resolve. This discovery altered their approach, urging them to maintain an unwavering spirit of determination and hope, even in the face of overwhelming odds.

Their final confrontation wasn't with a single, powerful entity, but a scattered, diffuse force that manifested differently in each location. They battled corrupted creatures, fought against the manipulation of the very environment itself, and overcame their own fears and doubts. Damian's earth magic grew stronger, Anya's solar energy became a beacon of healing and protection, and Lyra's knowledge of ancient lore and rituals proved invaluable in containing and neutralizing the fragments.

The transformation wasn't only physical; it was spiritual and emotional. They learned to trust each other implicitly, their bond forged in the fires of adversity. Damian discovered a confidence he'd never known before, his physical strength complemented by his burgeoning magical abilities. Anya's unwavering optimism was a source of strength and healing, both for herself and those around her. Lyra's unwavering intellect and strategic thinking kept them alive and moving forward.

Their journey took months, testing their resolve, their skills, and their friendship to its very limits. They learned to anticipate the fragments' unpredictable behavior, adapting their strategies to suit the unique properties of each. The fragments themselves became teachers, forcing them to innovate, adapt, and evolve.

The final fragment, located deep within the ancient ruins of a forgotten city, proved to be the most challenging. It was a nexus point, the heart of the ancient one's power, a swirling vortex of darkness that threatened to consume everything in its path. Here, the combined might of Anya's healing power, Damian's earth magic, and Lyra's knowledge culminated in a final, epic confrontation.

They emerged victorious, but weary, their bodies scarred but their spirits unbroken. The world was safe, for now. But the experience had profoundly shaped them, leaving them forever changed. Their victory wasn't just a defeat of a single, malevolent entity; it was a new beginning, a new era, a testament to their resilience, courage, and the unbreakable bond they forged in the face of overwhelming darkness. Their vigil continued, their eyes always on the horizon, ready to face whatever challenges the future might bring. The world was safe, for now, but their fight for its future had only just begun. The scars they carried – physical and emotional – were badges of honor, symbols of their hard-won victory and a reminder that their journey, their shared destiny, was far from over.

The sun, a molten orb sinking below the horizon, cast long shadows across the plains. The air, once thick with the stench of decay and corrupted magic, now carried the scent of damp earth and pine. Anya, Damian, and Lyra stood on a gentle rise, overlooking the land they had saved. The scars of the battle were still visible – blackened trees stood as silent sentinels, a testament to the destructive power they had faced. Yet, beneath the ravaged landscape, a subtle, almost imperceptible shift had occurred. New shoots of grass pushed through the scorched earth, vibrant green against the backdrop of charcoal. A lone bird sang a melody of hope, its voice echoing in the stillness.

Damian, his hand resting gently on Anya's, felt a profound sense of peace settle over him. The wounds on his body, though still tender, were healing. The darkness that had consumed him during the final confrontation felt like a distant nightmare, a haunting memory fading into the background. He looked at Anya, her face etched with a quiet contentment that mirrored his own. Their bond, forged in the crucible of battle, had deepened, its strength surpassing even his initial understanding of its power. It was not just a romantic bond, but a profound spiritual connection, a shared understanding forged through shared hardship and triumph. He saw not just a lover in her eyes, but a kindred spirit, a warrior who stood beside him, shoulder to shoulder, facing any danger the future might hold.

Anya, ever the optimist, found herself reflecting not on the battles won, but on the future that lay ahead. The victory was hard-earned, and the scars served as a reminder of the price paid for peace. However, the sight of new life sprouting from the ashes filled her with a sense of renewed hope. The world was healing, and with it, so were its people. Her solar energy, depleted during the final confrontation, had begun to replenish itself, flowing through her veins like a river of life. She felt a surge of strength, not just physical, but spiritual. The darkness had been pushed back, but it hadn't been eradicated. Vigilance was still required. Their journey was far from over.

Lyra, usually the quietest of the three, spoke, her voice breaking the silence. "We've won this battle, but the war is far from over," she said, her eyes fixed on the distant horizon. "The ancient one may be gone, but the shadows still linger. New threats will undoubtedly emerge." She picked up a small, smooth stone, its surface cool to the touch. It was a fragment of the obsidian spire, a memento of their battle in the desolate mountain pass. It pulsed faintly with residual energy, a subtle reminder of the power they had faced. "This isn't the end," she continued, her voice gaining strength. "It's a new beginning. A new chapter in the ongoing struggle between light and darkness."

The ensuing months brought a sense of uneasy calm. The land began to heal, the scars of battle slowly fading. Villages that had been ravaged by the ancient one's power were rebuilt, stronger and more resilient. The people, once consumed by fear and despair, found renewed hope. Anya, with her healing abilities, traveled from village to village, tending to the wounded, both physically and emotionally. Damian, his earth magic now a powerful tool, helped rebuild homes and infrastructure, restoring the land to its former glory. Lyra dedicated her time to studying ancient texts, searching for clues to future threats, and training a new generation of mages to safeguard the land.

Their work was not limited to physical restoration. They also focused on rebuilding the social fabric of their communities, strengthening the connections between people, and fostering a sense of unity and mutual support. They established schools and workshops, where people could learn new skills and trades, ensuring that their communities would remain self-sufficient and resilient in the face of future challenges. They worked tirelessly, fueled by their shared desire for a peaceful future, and a deep understanding of the fragility of peace.

They were constantly on alert, monitoring subtle shifts in the mystical energy fields of the land. The faint whispers of lingering dark energy kept them constantly vigilant. They were no longer fighting a singular, powerful entity; they were now facing a more insidious threat: the ever-present potential for new darkness to rise. Their victory was not a complete eradication of evil, but a hard-won respite, a temporary reprieve.

One evening, as they sat by a crackling fire, sharing stories and laughter, a subtle tremor ran through the ground. A wave of unease washed over them. They knew, instinctively, that this was not a natural occurrence. Lyra's eyes flashed with concern as she looked up at the stars, her gaze searching the heavens for any signs of disruption. They knew, in their hearts, that the shadows were still out there, waiting for an opportunity to rise again.

The peace they had achieved was not absolute, and the future was uncertain. Yet, they held onto hope, not as blind faith, but as a conscious choice, a determination to forge a better future for themselves and the world they had saved. The victory over the ancient one had been costly, but it had also strengthened their resolve, and deepened their bonds. They faced the future together, as a team, ready to face whatever challenges lay ahead.

Their vigilance never wavered. They continued to patrol the land, their senses honed to detect any sign of returning darkness. They established a network of informants, spreading their reach across the kingdom, ensuring that any potential threat would be detected early. They knew that the shadows would always be there, lurking in the darkness, but they were ready. They had the skills, the knowledge, and above all, the unbreakable bond that bound them together.

Anya discovered a deeper understanding of her solar magic, learning to channel its energy not only for healing and protection, but also for divination, allowing them to anticipate potential threats before they manifested. Damian's mastery over earth magic grew, his control becoming so refined that he could sense the slightest disturbances in the earth's energy. Lyra continued her relentless pursuit of knowledge, delving deeper into ancient texts, uncovering forgotten lore that helped them understand the nature of darkness and develop new strategies to combat it.

Their lives were no longer defined by the battles they had fought, but by the peace they had fought so hard to maintain. The constant threat of renewed conflict hung in the air, a silent pressure that never truly disappeared. Yet, they refused to let fear dictate their lives. Instead, they chose hope, courage, and the unwavering strength of their bond. They built their lives not on the foundation of past victories, but on the foundation of their unwavering determination to create a future free from the clutches of darkness. The peace they enjoyed was hard-won, but it was a peace they would fiercely protect. Their journey had changed them, but it had also given them something even more precious: a shared purpose, a profound bond, and the unshakeable knowledge that, together, they could face any challenge that the future might bring. The peaceful future they envisioned was not a passive acceptance of serenity; it was a future they actively created, day by day, with unwavering hope and courage. Their fight for a peaceful future had just begun.

Appendix

This appendix contains supplementary materials related to the world of Damien's Blood Moon, including maps of the key locations mentioned in the story, a detailed lineage of the ancient one's followers, and additional information on the various magical systems utilized by the characters.

Ancient One: The malevolent entity responsible for the events in the book. Possessed immense power derived from corrupted sources.

Solar Magic: A type of magic drawn from the sun, typically used for healing and offensive purposes.

Earth Magic: Magic harnessed from the earth, often employed for defense, construction, and manipulating the terrain.

Obsidian Spire: A massive structure, central to the Ancient One's power, constructed from dark magic and obsidian.

Whispers of Dark Energy: Subtle disturbances in the magical energy fields, indicating the presence of lingering dark magic.

While this story is entirely fictional, I drew inspiration from various mythological and historical sources, including Celtic mythology, Norse sagas, Native American Skin Walkers. These sources provided a rich background and a springboard for my imagination, helping to craft a compelling and believable world.

Jamie Scott is a fantasy author with a passion for action-packed plots and intriguing supernatural elements. A lifelong lover of storytelling, He began crafting fantastical tales at a young age, initially filling notebooks with intricate worlds and unforgettable characters. After years of honing their craft, He is thrilled to finally share this story with the world. When not lost in the worlds of their imagination, He can be found Hanging out with his family, and working hard to support them . He is currently working on the sequel to Damien's *Blood Moon*.